THE FIFTH PLANE

THE ONE THAT GOT AWAY

Vol 1.

A Novel

By

Val Walker

AMERICAN
BOOK PUBLISHER

Dedication

TO EVERYDAY HEROES

AND THE FLIGHT CREWS OF 9/11

Val Walker

Acknowledgements

To CORY. Thank you for being the kind, wise and amazing man and son you are. You are my unsung hero.

STEPHEN TRYON - AKA/PES. You always had my '6 as a FAM, friend and a crucial source of security information during the days I was flying following 9/11. My technical advisor before, during and after writing The 5th Plane. My BFF friend for life.

USAF Lt. COLONEL AHMED RAGHEB A wise and patient friend. Fellow Red Star pilot, artist, poet and USAF Lt. Colonel. Thank you for your time and patience in helping me understand. Gone too soon. You are missed by all.

WESTERN and DELTA AIRLINES. Thank you for giving me the profession of my dreams, the experiences of a lifetime and the unique and wonderful crews to share them with.

RIP Captain Pat Gilmore. 3/20/1947 – 9/2/2025

BILL and JERRI MELLAS, LAURA and ELLEN. My extended family who chose me for theirs. The Memoir Writer's Group. Thank you for your unwavering love and support during the writing of The 5th Plane.

To my dad CLINT WALKER who was and still is an inspiration and guiding light to millions of people worldwide. His legacy lives on through all of us whose lives he touched.

About the Author

DAL Captain Valerie Walker was flying Delta Boeing 767s and 757s out of Boston and New York JFK all month during September of 2001. September 11th was her day off. Her next flight on September 14th was one of a handful of airliners allowed to fly again shortly after 9/11 had shut down the skies over America. New York's River visual approach took her flight between the illuminated beauty of the Statue of Liberty on her Left and the smoldering ruins of the twin Towers on their right. The smell of death permeated the cockpit, breaking their hearts and strengthening their resolve." Never again. Not on our watch."

Val has written over 156 articles as managing editor, Art Director and flight test pilot for Plane & Pilot, Air Racing and Air Progress magazines, as well as Rotor & Wing and ALPA magazines. A first-degree Black Belt in Kenpo Karate, and student of Kendo, Wing Chun, Jiu-Jitsu and Krav Maga, she teaches defense for flight Crews and owns Raptor Tactical Martial Arts. Her Police

Aerial Patrol Helicopter pilot wings and badge were displayed in the Smithsonian as the first female police aerial patrol helicopter pilot. Her Airline Pilot uniforms were displayed in the 99's Museum and other museums across the US as one of the first 6 US female airline pilots and charter member of ISA +21. Valerie was hired by Western, now Delta, Air Lines on March 8, 1976 in their first class of airline pilots with a female pilot in it.

After 9/11 Captain Walker applied for and was chosen as one of the first 40 airline pilots to be trained in FLETC and deputized to secretly carry a firearm and fight terrorists attempting to enter the cockpit. You can find many articles and videos about her online. People Magazine, ALPA magazine, The LA Times and other publications have followed her throughout her career.

She is a member of the National Aviation and Space Writers Association, the Aviation Writers Club, The 99's, The Whirley Girls and a Charter member of ISA+21. Her pilot Certificates include Flight Engineer / commercial single and multiengine / helicopter-rotorcraft / CFI / Instrument / seaplane and Airline Transport ratings. She is rated to fly Captain on the DC-3/ B737/B727/B757/B767.

Captain Walker is a member of the Red Star Pilots Association and owns and flies her Chinese military Nanchang CJ-6, donating aerobatic rides for charities.

Val lives happily in Utah and enjoys hiking with her Akita Ashi, skiing, reading, writing, painting, working with raptors at Hawk Watch, riding horses and motorcycles with her friends. She plays classical guitar, kayaks and enjoys friends, family, small miracles and each new adventure life has to offer. Of the two wolves fighting inside us, she chooses to feed the good wolf.

Table of Contents

Chapter One
Follow the Leader

Feb. 19, 2001 / 10:43 pm PST / on final approach to Seattle Tacoma International Airport

"I'm not afraid of crashing…my secret is, just before we hit the ground, I jump as high as I can."

- Bill Cosby

Screams echoed in the passenger cabin. Sounds of shattering glass were followed by something big crashing against the cockpit door. First Officer Kelly Hunter winced and squinted into the darkness ahead. Another series of jolts accelerated to a washboard ride of increasing violence. She yanked her shoulder harnesses tighter and braced against the hurricane-force winds that boiled up to meet them. Fighting the controls took all of Kelly's concentration. Her focus narrowed to keeping the 767 right-side-up without tearing the wings off. Captain Bill Granger clung to the armrests, sheet white and overwhelmed by what he'd gotten them into. Captain Granger was fresh out of training and had amassed a total of 12 flight hours in an actual Boeing 767. His First Officer, Kelly Hunter, had been flying them for 5 years. Wisely, he had given his more experienced co-pilot control of the airplane. Unwisely, he'd pulled rank on Kelly and insisted they continue the flight into Seattle despite the severe turbulence, icing and 115 knot / 132 mph wind warnings.

The bludgeoning never let up and it was getting worse. Ten thousand feet over Puget Sound two hundred tons of metal and humanity were fighting for survival. A cold river of arctic air fell out of the jet stream and rushed down to engulf them. When it struck, the 767 dropped as if the air had been yanked out from under them. The 767 was just a tiny speck of light in the black maw of the storm. Then the turbulence hit again, hard.

Kelly's sweat-slicked hand flew off the throttle. Instinctively, she fumbled for the power levers again and clung to them. The screams had stopped now, drowned in a dark place beyond fear. They were still trapped in a roiling cataract of falling air.

"Bill! Kill the engine heat. We need the power!" Kelly didn't know if the captain heard her or not. It was like being inside God's Kettle drum. The stall-warning clattered, shaking the controls and adding a snare-drum effect to the Hellish tympani.

Panting with effort, Kelly shoved the power up and locked the yoke in both hands. They were falling. Whether the stick-shaker's machine-gun bursts were rattling a real stall warning or not was anyone's guess. It just added to the pandemonium in the cockpit.

The next updraft jammed the passengers into their seats. The plane slowly began to claw its way back to flight altitude. The turbulence subsided to a moderate rattle. Kelly realized she'd been holding her breath and sucked in a mouthful of air. It tasted of Ozone and fear. Maybe the worst was over.

Alarm shot through her body when a violent updraft hit the left wing, threatening to roll them onto their back. Kelly jammed in opposite rudder and full aileron. People who sat on the right had a horrifying view of lights where they shouldn't have been as the 767 continued to roll, then abruptly righted itself.

"Jesus!" It was both a curse and a prayer. The captain's fingers dug into the armrests. At this point he was just along for the ride. Kelly didn't have time to look. She knew what he was thinking. *We're not going to make it.*

Another jolt shook the plane. Kelly's eyes burned as she fought to stay in control. A sickening rush of dread coiled up her spine. One glance at the captain and panic threatened to engulf her. *Bill was in full "Deer in the headlights" mode.* She couldn't expect any help from him. Another blast whipsawed the aircraft's tail back and forth horizontally, throwing them against the sides of the cockpit. *How much more could the 767 take before it began to break up?* Kelly inhaled through clenched teeth and denied herself the luxury of falling apart. Her jaw tightened in grim determination. *They were not going to die. Not tonight, and not on her watch.* She leaned forward and peered through the torrent of water. Indistinct, but there, Seattle's runway lights grew brighter and streamed across the windscreen. If not for their seat belts the next disorienting hit would have slammed them against the ceiling. Rain hammered the cockpit like rocks being shot into a tin roof. "Give me wipers Bill!" The captain clung to his chair mesmerized by the blurred needles of the flight instruments. The indicators were moving too fast to make any sense.

"Bill!" Kelly risked a hand to grab his shoulder and shook him. "Give me some wipers. NOW!"

He looked at her. Then he reached up, steadied his arm with his other hand and captured the switch. Screeching wiper blades flailed a path through the deluge. The distant patch of lights began to look more like a runway and less like a child's crazed kaleidoscope of color. Kelly clung to the lights like a lifeline and kept the 767 on an oscillating descent toward them. Another series of gusts battered the airplane. The last drops of Kelly's coffee made a suicidal leap over the lip of her cup. It joined the cold sweat that soaked her shirt.

"Gear down! Set flaps to thirty!" Wind raked the skin of the airplane and drowned out the whine of the actuators. A reassuring thump announced the last phase of flight as the huge wheels dropped and locked in place.

Back in the cabin a sour smell of vomit permeated everything. Unsecured luggage leapt from the overhead bins against a cacophony of rattles and shrieks. Strangers shared wild-eyed stares, thinking thoughts they didn't want to put into words. They'd given up looking for reassurance in the faces of the flight attendants. Their eyes mirrored the same terror.

Up front, Kelly struggled with the flight controls. She willed the 767 to stay on course. Houses, lights, and cars drew closer as they thrashed their way down the glide path. She had to shout to be heard. "Call out wind shear for me Bill!" Taking her attention away from the approaching terrain wasn't an option. The cliff wall that Seattle Tacoma's runway 16R sat on top of loomed up out of the darkness. Runway lights on top of the cliff glowed enticingly. Bait for downdrafts she suspected would be created by the 115 knot winds plunging off of the approach end of SEA /TAC's runway 16R.

Bill clung to the checklist. "Five hundred feet above touchdown!" He pressed the headset to his ear to hear the controller. "Cleared to land. Winds are steady at a hundred and fifteen knots."

Things were happening faster now. They always did seconds from touchdown. Kelly went on high alert mentally and physically. Her world shrank to include nothing but the rain-slicked stripes of the runway threshold that rushed toward them. She instinctively felt where the wheels were and the sink rate of the massive 767 as it slowed beneath her. Then the left wing jerked viciously upward and the 767's tail swung left. The nose slewed far to the right of the centerline. Kelly had an alarming view of the runway as it rotated past the cockpit and disappeared behind Captain Granger's profile. She muscled in full left aileron and rudder. Nothing happened. The wing remained in a high bank and they were still turning right. There was nothing she could do about it. Her control play was maxed out. Kelly slid her palm to the go-around switches and prepared for a missed approach. It was her only choice, and not a good one. They were pointed at a radio tower.

The wing suddenly dropped and leveled out again. The nose swung back to the centerline and the aircraft gentled into a glide toward the touchdown lights. Kelly relaxed her grip, flared and went for the landing.

"Two hundred feet above touchdown!" Bill's voice had a desperate pitch to it. They both knew they couldn't take another hit this close to the ground. Kelly slowed her closure rate and prayed. *Please let it stay calm for another five seconds.* Someone must have heard her. Eight massive Goodyear tires met the asphalt like a first kiss. The big bird settled onto its landing gear and transferred 400,000 pounds of metal, fuel and flesh from the wings to the runway.

Kelly pulled the power to idle and yanked in the thrust reversers. The battered 767 roared its defiance into the storm and shuddered to a stop on the runway. A loose cargo pod cart-wheeled past them and banged its way into the darkness. The cockpit was quiet except for an electronic hum and the wind howling outside. They sat in stunned silence for a moment as gusts rocked the plane.

Then the cabin P.A. crackled to life with a Flight Attendant's shaken voice. "Welcome to Seattle-Tacoma International Airport. And that, ladies and gentlemen, is why the pilots make the big bucks!" Kelly sank into her seat and flushed at the round of applause outside the cockpit door. *Irrational anger usually followed in the aftermath of blind fear. Not gratitude.* She pried her cramped fingers off the throttles and let out a long sigh.

"You don't hear that very often. A flight attendant publicly acknowledging we earn our pay." The humor of the situation suddenly struck her. "It must be the Stockholm syndrome."

Captain Granger let go of his armrest. "I sure feel like I earned my pay tonight. All I want to do is get out of here and go to the hotel." Kelly skewered him with a look of utter disbelief, her diplomacy fading. She undid her shoulder harness and leaned in.

"Just one thing Bill…"

"What's that?"

Her words were succinct. "We shouldn't have attempted this tonight. I told you I wanted to wait it out at an alternate airport." Kelly was smiling but her eyes meant business. "I don't care if it IS book-legal or if everybody else is doing it because the airport's still open. If you ever insist on flying into severe turbulence, icing and winds like this again I will hit you in the head with the crash ax and take over."

He glared at her in surprise. Then a shamefaced look of realization softened his worn features. "I'd appreciate that."

Kelly relaxed. She almost laughed at his "guilty-as-charged" expression. "In that case captain – I'd follow you anywhere." This time the smile was reflected in her eyes.

He grinned sheepishly, took the controls and craned his neck to find an exit.

"Let's get off this runway before some other fool tries to land on us. They're still shooting approaches."

The sound of accelerating jet engines thundered overhead. "Seattle tower this is American 129 executing a missed approach. There's severe turbulence on final. We're unable to control the aircraft. Shut this airport down NOW!"

"Roger that American 129. You're cleared for the missed approach. Attention all aircraft, SEATAC is now closed to all arriving and departing flights."

Kelly had an irrational urge to duck when the less fortunate jet roared past overhead. Bill worked the throttles and gingerly maneuvered their big machine off the runway, careful not to let the wind slip under the wing. They glanced at each other in silent agreement. *They had been lucky to make it in.*

The harsh glare of halogen lights at their arrival gate had never looked so welcoming. The wind still screamed like a Banshee and rocked the jetway as the Gate agent tried to coax it into position. Kelly and Bill completed the shutdown checklists and dragged their bags out of their restraints. Kelly took a moment to give the control column a furtive pat. The beatings these machines could take and keep going never ceased to impress her. She murmured a muffled "Thanks baby." under her breath and followed the captain out the door. The exhausted passengers and crew staggered into the terminal. Grateful the awful experience was finally over.

At the adjacent gate Mohammed Atta raised his head and glowered at the flight status board with bloodshot eyes. He and Marwan had arrived from Atlanta and been waiting in the Seattle terminal for three hours, only to have the American Airlines flight their Jihadi cell members were on make a missed approach and go to Portland. Atta stood up and pulled at the grungy tackiness of his pants. He spoke without looking at Marwan.

"They will bus in tomorrow. We will wait at the hotel." Relieved, Marwan got up and gathered his belongings.

"It has been a long day Mohammed. They know where to find us." He looked at his friend's pallid complexion and sunken eyes. The long months of plotting, arguing with Osama bin Laden and pushing their luck were starting to take their toll. Tonight, Atta just looked brittle. Like he could shatter at any moment and it frightened Marwan.

Atta watched the motley exodus of people pour out of the adjoining gate area. *Why had this Delta flight made it in when the American flight he waited for hadn't?* It was just one more irritant in a demanding day of air travel. Atta had started his day on the East Coast in BWI on a Delta flight from there to Atlanta Georgia. Atta and Marwan had connected in Atlanta and caught an earlier flight into Seattle to meet other members of his cell here. Marwan followed as Atta trailed the last of the passengers into the concourse. Atta's mind wandered to the logistics of gathering the others together tomorrow. He walked a robotic path behind the black uniform boots of the person in front of him. Like him, they were dragging a flight crew bag. The mob of people slowed for the escalator and he looked up at a long flaxen braid. It snaked incongruously out from under a pilot's hat. Bile from the piece of greasy pizza he'd eaten earlier burned in his throat as he struggled to control the expression of outrage that was spreading across his face. *The woman is wearing a man's uniform doing a job only a man should do. She was the personification of everything they'd come to America to destroy.* Atta's nails bit into the palms of his hands. Something inside him snapped. *She was an abomination.*

"Mohammed?" Marwan's hand on his shoulder brought him back to reality. Atta hadn't realized that he'd stopped. His whole body was trembling with rage as he stared at the pilot. Shaken at his loss of control, Atta forced himself to relax and reassure his friend.

"It is nothing. I am just tired." Marwan almost looked convinced as he followed Atta down the escalator behind the tall woman in the uniform. One step higher than she was, Atta glared at the back of Kelly's head. Then a strange expression flickered across his features and he shuddered as a wave of elation swept through him. *It was clear why Allah had brought him to this place, making him wait.* A thin smile pulled at his mouth and stretched into a demented thing. *Allah was speaking directly to him, his holy warrior, giving Atta a divine Fatwa.* The thrill was powerful. Almost sensual. He looked at the back of Kelly's head with renewed resolve. *She would be an example of what happens to women who defy the laws of Islam.* He could almost feel himself sitting behind her in the cockpit, slitting her throat. *His death as a martyr to Islam would have even greater glory when it was written in the history of the new Caliphate.* He looked at the female again with a strange mix of revulsion and covetousness.

When the escalator reached the baggage claim she and her captain headed toward the Mayflower Hotel pick-up area. The same hotel where Atta and his cell members were staying. Any doubts about the divine directive left Atta as he marveled at the fluke. Their mission at the hotel was to steal the uniforms and credentials of flight crews.

The pilot turned to pull something from her pocket. Atta was quick to note the name on her ID badge. "Kelly Hunter." He slowed his breathing and turned to face Marwan, blocking his route to the hotel van.

"We will wait for the next bus." Marwan looked perplexed but did not question his leader's reasons. Feeling uncharacteristically benevolent Atta sat down on a bench and motioned his friend to sit beside him. "The first bus is too crowded. I will tell you the rest later." Atta's features settled into a ruthless mask. "It is perfect."

Chapter Two
Something Evil

Feb 19, 2001 / 1:32 pm EST / enroute from BWI to Atlanta Hartsfield International Airport, Ga. / Earlier that day

"Keep your friends close and your enemies closer."

-   Michael Corleone, The Godfather II

The American Airlines pilot sitting in the cockpit behind Delta Captain Pat Gilmore was just creepy. There was no other word to describe it. He made the Delta captain uneasy about sharing the jumpseat with this particular pilot from another carrier. The guy was dressed in an American Airlines pilot uniform with an American Airlines pilot ID badge. When he wasn't asking questions about how to fly the plane, he was staring sullenly at the backs of their necks. Gilmore shrugged his shoulders as if something evil had sunken its teeth into him. Then he glanced at his co-pilot. Dean's angular profile was bent over the navigation unit. The control yokes moved in response to commands he was entering into the autopilot. Gilmore swiveled in his seat and faced the jumpseat rider. He forced himself to look into those flat dead eyes.

"So what type of equipment do you fly at American?"

"This kind." The man pulled his lips back from his teeth in a parody of a grin. An odd answer but it was a start. Gilmore pressed on.

"Do you mean you fly the Boeing 767 and 757?"

"Yes."

The captain looked over at his co-pilot and saw the same question mirrored in his eyes.

"If you're a pilot on the 767 and 757 at American why are you asking so many questions about how we fly them?"

"We fly them differently at American. I am curious about your procedures." He turned his back on the captain and took an interest in the East Coast of North Carolina passing 37,000 feet below them, signaling an end to the conversation. A vein began to throb in Gilmore's left temple. The man's answers were vague and evasive. He had effectively dismissed the captain in his own cockpit.

"A 767 flies like a 767 no matter what airline you work for." Gilmore persisted. "Your procedures can't be that different."

"At American, they are different." The words were spoken slowly into the window. The man's cadaverous features were reflected there, a mask of disdain.

Gilmore had a sudden urge to get up and throttle the jump-seating pilot, or shove him out of the cockpit. He wanted to get to Atlanta fast and be rid of him. The man's whole demeanor smacked of arrogance and contempt and his answers were just strange. *What the Hell was going on?* Gilmore wondered. He took a deep breath and calmed himself. His methodical nature needed a sensible explanation. He found it in the pilot's swarthy Middle Eastern features and strong accent. *The man's obviously not from here.* he thought. *Maybe I'm losing something in the translation.* Gilmore turned back to the business of flying. He felt better as he settled into the comforting routine of checklists and crew management.

"Ok Dean. I've got the airplane now".

"You've got the airplane captain. I've got the radios." Dean flipped a switch and the cockpit's speakers crackled to life.

"Delta 2210 contact Atlanta Center on one-three-two decimal two-five."

"Roger Washington Center one-three-two decimal two-five."

"What are you doing there now? Is that the autopilot turning us or are you doing it?" The thick accent intruded on their mental sanctuary, an unpleasant reminder that he was still there. Captain Gilmore squeezed his eyes shut. The muscles of his jaw flexed over bone as he spoke.

"We have three levels of automation. This is the second." He wanted to scream *Don't you know that you idiot?* Captain

Gilmore gathered his wits and diplomacy. "I'm using the second level with the control knob to intercept the radial." He punched the Lateral Navigation button. "Now I'm going to the third level where the autopilot assumes control."

Dean rolled his eyes.

"What kind of autopilot systems are you guys at American using anyway?" Gilmore asked. He knew that whatever it was it couldn't be so different that an airline pilot would have trouble understanding the basics of what was going on.

"A different one." The American pilot was leaning between them now, his rank breath marking his territory.

Gilmore refused to look at the man. All Boeing 767s came equipped with the same autopilot. *Maybe if I pretend he isn't there the jump seat rider will get the hint.* Dean raised his hands and shook his head as if to say "Leave me out of this one". Gilmore reached into his flight case and pulled out a high-altitude navigation chart, hoping to send a signal that he was too busy to be disturbed. It had the opposite effect.

"You do not need those to navigate this aircraft do you?"

The captain stuffed the map back into his flight case and turned to face his tormentor. "No, but we always use them as a backup." He made himself look into the flat black eyes again. "You're not a U.S. Citizen, are you?" The eyes hardened as if the man thought he'd been insulted.

"No."

"Where are you from?"

"I am Egyptian." the pilot stated. "I came here to fly."

Captain Gilmore ran his fingers through his receding hairline. Every time he thought this man couldn't get any more puzzling he was proven wrong. If the jump seat rider wasn't wearing an American Airlines ID badge with his name and photograph on it Gilmore would have suspected that he wasn't an airline pilot at all. His brow furrowed trying to make sense of it.

What kind of people are they hiring over there anyway? He wondered. More importantly, who was this guy riding behind him?

"You've got the airplane for a minute Dean. I'm going to gab with Mohammed for a bit."

The captain rested his arm on the top of his seatback and attempted a casual smile. "So Mr. Atta," he said, repeating the name listed on the pilot's ID badge. "I didn't think a foreign national could get an Airline Transport Rating here in the United States."

"Yes we can." Atta sounded confident.

Dean was monitoring the airplane but he was also listening to the exchange between his captain and the unsavory American Airlines pilot. "Uh, captain." he interjected. "I think they can get an ATP here. We train Foreign Nationals from all over the world, including military pilots. Then they go back and fly for Air Carriers in their own countries."

"Oh. I didn't know that." Gilmore admitted. "Well, I guess I learn something new every day."

Atta's thin slice of a mouth stretched into a sanctimonious smile. "Yes you did learn, didn't you?"

Gilmore felt like he'd been slapped. Atta's reply brought a sudden surge of anger and he had to wrestle it down. The two men stared at each other for a moment before the captain shook himself out of it. *What's the matter with me?* he thought disgustedly. *It's just a social exchange. The man's an incompetent idiot to boot. You have an airplane to fly.* Captain Gilmore broke the staring contest by looking out the window.

Gilmore worried that he might be overreacting. He took a sip of coffee from his Styrofoam cup and realized he wasn't. Something was wrong. He turned back to Atta, intent on another round.

"How did you get hired by American Airlines?" he asked. "American Air Carriers don't hire Foreign Nationals even if they do have an ATP."

The co-pilot turned in his seat to look at the two combatants and chimed in again. "I've got to agree with the captain on this one Mohammed." Dean banked the 767 to dodge an ominous-looking thunderhead. "I didn't think we hired Foreign Nationals as pilots either."

Atta glared at the two men. Then he smiled.

"Obviously you are both very wrong." he lied, holding out the ID Badge. "That has changed. Your President Bush has made it law that all people must have equal job opportunities here in the United States whether they are citizens or not. Otherwise," he smirked "how could I be here?"

The sheer audacity of that reply and the threat of racial prejudice made both men doubt themselves. Atta took advantage of the breach and continued. "Your President Bush wants all foreign Air Carriers to fly in the United States, competing with your own companies. He is making laws that other countries can even buy your airlines." He hesitated, unable to deny himself the luxury of the next uncontrolled words as they spilled out. "You are not smart to think that I cannot fly for an American airline."

Atta looked at the outraged faces of the Americans and couldn't resist one more barb.

"It is a stupid question." he finished.

The co-pilot turned back to his tasks. *This was bad. The strange little man had no sense of propriety and was determined to create a problem. At least one pilot had to keep his mind clear and fly the airplane. Something was obviously wrong with the rider.* The captain's voice was unnervingly soft when he spoke.

"It's not a stupid question. What is stupid is you sitting on my jump seat being rude and interrupting us when we're busy. Riding in the cockpit is a privilege not a right. If I didn't have a full plane right now I'd send you back to ride in coach between the fat guy and two screaming kids. You're way out of line buddy."

Atta sat like a stone, calculating what his self-indulgence might have cost him. Then he swallowed his pride and lied again. He comforted himself with the mental image of ripping out the big meddling Captain's throat.

"It was not meant to offend you." he forced himself to say. "Perhaps the differences in our cultures have caused a misunderstanding."

The captain didn't think so but it was obviously the best attempt the man could make at an apology. *Why does he keep staring at my throat while he's talking?* Gilmore brought his hand up and rubbed his neck, flicking his eyes to the clock. *Only forty more minutes and he'll be out of here.* Gilmore thought. For some reason he did not want to turn his back on the man.

"I'm not unfamiliar with your culture." the captain replied. "I flew C-130s for the military out of Bahrain during the Gulf War. It's a beautiful country." The look he got from Atta convinced him that he'd made a big mistake in his choice of subject matter. A wall came down. Atta's eyes went black and his face looked like a death mask. At this point it was worse to look at him than to turn his back on him. In the silence that followed both the first officer and the captain concentrated on flying the 767, determined to get to Atlanta with no more distractions.

Atta watched the pilots intently, his mind storing anything he could use to find and hit a target accurately with the big jet. He took notes as the two Delta pilots deviated around lines of thunderstorms and began their descent into Atlanta. It was getting busy now. This was the phase of flight where Atta would gather his most useful information. He leaned forward, looking over the captain's shoulder.

"When you set the speed with the manual knob does that override the programmed speed?" he asked. "Will the autopilot still descend to the programmed target?"

The captain twitched at the rank ketosis of Atta's breath and Atta's voice so close to his ear. The increasing workload of descending into Atlanta had almost allowed him to forget that Atta was still there.

"Yes. It overrides the programmed speed." he responded impatiently. "The aircraft should still go to the programmed runway unless you mess with the Lateral Navigation function or put it on heading." It was easier to answer the inane questions than to argue with the man. Weather deviations, trying to get a word in edgewise to approach control and looking out for dozens of other aircraft that were trying to do the same thing took total concentration. Gilmore thought his last discussion with Atta about cockpit interruptions had been painfully clear. Apparently not. He jerked a laminated page from the glare shield pocket and called out "Descent Checklist." Gilmore felt Atta's hand on the back of his seat as the man leaned forward. "If I set in a speed that exceeds the airplane's limits will the autopilot still fly it?"

The captain pointed at his altimeter which was unwinding through fifteen thousand feet. "I don't know how you guys at American work your policies but at Delta we have a sterile cockpit below eighteen thousand feet. That means no talking unless it's us working our checklists." He turned his head and found himself almost nose to nose with Atta.

"You need to be quiet now." the captain said in a voice that brooked no argument.

"Altimeters?" the co-pilot asked hopefully.

The two men stared at each other for a long moment before Atta dropped his eyes and the captain turned back to the business at hand. "Two-niner niner-two." he responded, grateful to be back in familiar territory. *Just a few more minutes now.* he promised himself.

"Delta 2210 this is Atlanta Approach Control. Keep your speed up."

Dean glanced at Captain Gilmore and answered the radio call. "How fast will you let us go?" Gilmore looked hopeful.

On the ground in Atlanta the redneck working at Approach Control tapped his headset with his finger. "That's one for the record." he said to the ATC controller seated next to him. "They usually complain when we ask them to speed it up." He spat an over-chewed wad of gum into an empty Cup 'O Noodles carton and tracked the green blip on his radar scope. "Delta 2210 Heavy you're number one for the approach. I have a whole line of aircraft behind you. You can go as fast as you want."

"Roger that." Dean responded, receiving a nod from Gilmore "We'll keep the speed up."

The burly captain ran the throttles up and pointed the nose toward Atlanta. "We'll hold the gear and flaps until we're 3 miles out." Dean nodded in agreement, unaware that he was leaning forward in his seat willing the jet toward the airport.

Atta scribbled furiously in his notebook, engrossed in his mission again. The stress of evading detection these last few months had frayed his machine-like detachment. Allah willing, his lapse in judgment taunting the pilots would not come back to haunt him. He glanced up as Gilmore set a lower altitude in the autopilot and inserted the command for a faster speed. Atta grunted in satisfaction. That procedure would be useful.

The 767's outline swelled from a dot to a football in the Tower windows as it sped toward the runway. It slowed at the last minute and dropped gear and flaps with air-show precision. The controller raised his binoculars. "Delta 2210 heavy you are cleared for a long landing runway 27 Right as requested." A nice gap had opened between the Delta jet and a long line of landing lights descending behind them. The knot in the Tower controller's stomach vanished. He looked at the bottle of Pepto-Bismol in his hand and set it back down. The next thirty minutes wouldn't be spent herding a swarm of hornets after all. He felt generous. "Good job, Delta."

"Thanks." Dean could feel the man in the jump seat staring at them again. "We're cleared for the long landing and requesting permission to roll through the high-speed exit into the ramp for gate Alpha 30."

The tower controller felt giddy with relief at the break. Delta's rapid rollout would net him even more airspace. "Are you guys having an emergency you haven't told us about or do you have a hot date here in Atlanta?"

"We just want to get to the gate." Dean's eyes were fixed on the landing zone.

"Roger Delta. You're cleared for the long landing and taxi as requested."

Atta looked away from the pilots and used his last minutes in the cockpit to note where the crash axe, door lock and viewport were. His bloodless lips stretched in an ironic grimace. *Knowing how to land a 767 was of no importance to the mission, just a small personal point of pride. He was, after all, an engineer by profession.* He took a few notes anyway. His pen jerked an inky scrawl across the page as the wheels hit the runway. Atta looked at the notebook, flipped to a new page and wrote it again leaning into the turn as the jet swerved onto the taxiway. Thinly muffled thumps, bells and P.A. announcements vibrated through the cockpit door as the flight attendants rushed through their after-landing checklist, caught off guard by the short taxi. Captain Gilmore and Dean maneuvered toward the gate with a single mind while completing their checklists and radio calls.

The ground crew waiting to guide them in looked uncertain as the charging 767 rounded the corner. They relaxed when Gilmore pulled both engines to idle and shut one down. The big jet slowed and lumbered gently into the gate. Dean and Gilmore finished their checklists, pointedly ignoring Atta. The last engine had barely whined itself to a stop when a gate agent opened the passenger cabin door. Atta continued sitting in his seat watching the pilots. They could hear passengers battling with luggage and vying for the "first-out" position.

Captain Gilmore got out of his chair, wedged himself past Atta and opened the cockpit door. "You need to leave now." he stated, gesturing toward the stampede of deplaning passengers. Atta slowly stood and picked up his bag. He glared at the captain and took his time moving out of the cockpit. Gilmore stayed by the door until Atta's rigid form disappeared into the maelstrom of departing travelers. Then he let his shoulders slump and took a deep breath. His whole body was still vibrating with anger and the need to hit something. Logic couldn't explain why he was having such a visceral reaction to the obnoxious little Egyptian or why he was so relieved to be rid of him.

"That was one creepy guy." Dean commented.

"My thoughts exactly." Gilmore slid back into his seat to pack up his flight case.

Chapter Three
Fear and Loathing

Feb. 19, 2001 / 2:32 EST / Atlanta Hartsfield International Airport, Atlanta, Ga. Earlier that day

"Instinct doesn't lie. People do."

-   Unknown

Atta left the Delta aircraft feeling like he'd rattled the tiger's cage and come away unscathed. He had nothing but contempt for these infidels and their creed of personal freedoms. Their freedoms would allow him to destroy them. Atta's features molded themselves in a scowl as he stalked through the terminal. Passengers avoided him and mothers instinctively positioned themselves between the man and their children when he passed. Dark frightening things radiated off him. He was a bad advertisement for American Airlines.

The squeaking wheel on his crew luggage was starting to wear on him. The cursed thing seemed like it was screaming a warning to everyone he passed. Calling attention to him. Revealing him for what he was. *He'd smear butter on it later.* It was an old trick a flight attendant had suggested. Atta looked at his watch and swallowed a creeping sense of urgency. He felt unclean and sullied from the time he'd been forced to spend away from his fellow Al Qaeda cell members. He forced his anxious mind to the pleasant fact that he'd gleaned useful information under the noses of airport security and the airlines. A rush of power thrilled through him. Again, he felt invincible, superior… worthy to sit at the right hand of Allah. His mind would not stop ping-ponging through the gamut of emotions. It disturbed him that he was feeling any emotions at all. Maybe he needed to eat something. He couldn't remember the last time he'd eaten. No matter. Atta suppressed the racing thoughts and concentrated on his next objective.

He caught the escalator to the shuttle that would take him to his next flight to Seattle. Atta forced his way to the front of the mob at the bottom of the escalator. It placed them in front of the arriving train. The shuttle's doors hissed open, disgorging one group of people as it inhaled Atta with another. An irritating recording of Darth Vader's voice threatened to amputate body parts if the passengers didn't immediately squeeze in tighter and clear the doors. The compartment hissed shut and the train lurched forward. Atta shoved an elderly woman's sweater aside and plopped down in the handicapped only area. He pulled out his dog-eared notepad and reviewed his next steps.

Attempting to ride in the cockpit of an American Airlines jet as a pilot was too risky. He could not bluff his way through questions there. He already knew what he had to do. They'd been doing it for months. *I will change into civilian clothes in the large men's room stall.* he thought. This time he would be sitting in the first-class section of an American Airlines jet as a passenger, watching the habits of the flight crews and evaluating vulnerabilities that could be used against them from the cabin.

He sighed and steadied himself against the seat, wondering why he suddenly felt weak. His body was demanding fuel again. *I despise this weak flesh.* Atta agonized. Something about denying his body what it needed made him feel holy, as if he lived in another otherworldly more sanctified place. His hands trembled from low blood sugar. The elderly lady next to him raised a frail hand as if to steady him. Atta's adder-like glare made her jerk her hand back, gather her sweater and retreat to the far side of the bench. Satisfied with his restored self-control, Atta spread out further and waited for the next concourse. The train screeched to a stop on another wave of canned instructions.

"The next stop is Terminal C. Please hold on. This train is stopping." Atta got up and pushed his way past people trying to get in. He dragged the noisy crew bag behind him and took the escalator to the gate where he entered the men's room. Pulling the packet of butter out of his uniform pocket, he closed the handicapped stall and knelt to smother the offending wheel with it. When he left he'd changed into civilian clothes and the roller bag was silent. He felt less vulnerable now.

Atta wiped an oily smear of butter on his pant leg and looked around for his Al Qaeda contact, Marwan Al-Shehhi.

Content to blindly follow Atta's lead, the stocky Jihadist was the closest thing he had to a friend. Atta spotted his roommate's unkempt head of curly black hair hunched over a flight schedule and strolled in his direction. For Marwan this planned attack on The Great Satan was all a grand adventure where the good guys killed the bad guys. Like his blind faith in Atta, Marwan never doubted that Allah would reward them all for the slaughter of infidels with an eternity of ecstasy. He rode the crest of an ebullient wave of religious fervor, striking a balance with Atta's pedantic hate of the West. In Islam religion and politics were inseparable.

Atta stopped a few feet away from Marwan and picked up a magazine. Marwan looked up and the two men acknowledged each other with a barely perceptible nod. Atta dropped his luggage in a seat between them and sat down. Marwan spoke softly and feigned indifference as he plucked a pen from his shirt pocket and ran it down a list of flight numbers.

"Did the examination go well Mohammed?" Marwan asked.

"Yes. And the others?" Atta opened the magazine. His lips barely moved. "Their studies are progressing according to the lesson plan?" He was referring to the teams of Al Qaeda members who were conducting similar surveillance on flights up and down the East Coast.

Marwan's attempt to quash a smile was unsuccessful. He enjoyed being Allah's action hero too much. "They are all doing well and learning much of value. I expect them to graduate soon." He turned to Atta with the flame of a Zealot illuminating his features. "I have much to tell you Mohammed. It is all so easy. You will be pleased." Across the aisle a woman glanced up and shuffled her cell phone to her other ear, annoyed at Marwan's rising voice.

Atta gave him a cautionary look. "We will discuss it back at the University." Cowed, Marwan lowered his eyes back to the flight schedule. The woman got up and moved to a distant side of the room. Atta flipped a magazine page and went on. "I have word from home that more professors should be arriving in time for graduation." The group needed two more pilots and Osama bin Laden had promised that they would have them.

Still perusing the schedule Marwan smiled again, a beatific expression on his face. The arrival of the others and the relative success they'd been experiencing indicated that Allah favored what they were doing. Marwan was already thinking of himself as a great martyr and saint of Islam. Atta crossed his legs and brought the magazine up.

Fifteen minutes later he glanced at his watch then at the flight schedule screen over the podium. Yellow letters flashed on their Seattle flight's departure time. His stomach clenched at the message: "Delayed." Atta's eyes strayed to the television monitor. The big red boxes and wind warnings on the CNN weather map hinted at the reason. He wiped a clammy hand across his face. *They had to get to Seattle tonight. The others were meeting them there.* He got up and took a seat closer to the screen. A chipper weather girl was waving an ominous hand over the Pacific Northwest. Atta strained to hear what she was saying.

"And the wild weather is expected to intensify later tonight. Dangerous winds rolled a semi-truck on the interstate between Portland and Seattle causing a ten-car pile-up. In the small community of Beaux Arts seventy-mile-an-hour gusts uprooted trees causing damage to cars and a home in the bay district. Airport delays are in effect for the area but no airport closures are expected." She smiled and moved on to rain on the East Coast. Atta glanced at the board again and felt a surge of relief. The flashing "delayed" message for their flight out of Atlanta to Seattle had been replaced with a new departure time thirty minutes later.

Marwan's concerned bulk moved into Atta's peripheral vision with a greasy Pizza Hut box. He sat it on the plastic seat beside his leader's ashen form. "Mohammed, until we meet in Paradise you must still eat."

Chapter Four
Abomination

Feb. 20, 2001 / 08:00am PST / Mayflower Hotel Seattle, WA.

"Hate is like acid. It damages the vessel in which it is stored."

- Ann Landers

There are things that are worse than death. Rasheed knows this because two of them are boring into the back of his skull. He swallows and watches the Lebanese maid disappear into the elevator. Then he turns to face Atta. The eyes that focus on him are black and vacant. Shark-like. They appraise him as if he's a piece of raw meat. Rasheed shakes the impression off, telling himself it's only Atta's determination as a holy warrior he sees there.

"It is done Mohammed." Rasheed says. "The maid will tell us if the pilot is still in her room." Atta grunts and turns on his heel to wait in another corner of the hotel. Rasheed sits on a convenient bench, concerned with his leader's sudden obsession with the female pilot.

The maid is a member of a different Al Qaeda cell based in Seattle. Her only task is to let Rasheed search the hotel rooms of flight crews. Atta's cell has been stealing credentials and uniforms to be used in future missions for two days now. Before last night, the pilot and flight attendant rooms had been picked at random.

Atta stared at the worn carpet in front of his shoes. His engineer's mind clicks through the possibilities like a machine. Half of him relishes his new plan. In a dark corner of his mind another voice is screaming that this is a big mistake. He is risking too much. Exposing them to scrutiny. For a moment Atta is appalled at his actions. Then he snarls at the weakness he finds in himself and slams the door of logic in the face of doubt. *It is an excellent plan!*

Atta found a chair in an inconspicuous corner of the lobby and sat down. It is reassuring to know that Rasheed is the only one the maid speaks with or sees.

This is the strength of Al Qaeda cells. Atta thinks. *If one is compromised it has no knowledge of the others.*

Atta knows Rasheed and Wail believe his decision to target the pilot is not a cautious one. What passes for a smile stretches his mouth across the pallid skin of his face. *The men's thoughts are of no consequence. They are like well-trained dogs. They will do as he says.*

He picks up a thumbed-through copy of the Seattle Times and finds himself wondering why he has stepped outside of his own carefully structured rules. Atta runs a hand over his face. The unrelenting pressures of the past few months squeeze his brain. *It is a divine edict.* he reassures himself. *It is a Fatwa that Allah has revealed to me. Allah had dragged the abomination of the female pilot across his nose last night for a reason.* Atta thought the choice was elegant and fitting. He waited.

On the third floor Kelly Hunter moaned and pulled a pillow over her head. The ice machine and elevator were trading clanks and chimes outside her room. Plodding feet and slamming doors joined the noise in a busy morning Samba. Seattle was awake and ready to meet the new day. Kelly wasn't. A moment of silence began to lull her back to sleep. She sighed and relaxed into the body heat of her covers.

"Housekeeping!" The dusky Lebanese maid pulled her cleaning cart out of the way and tried to sound cheerful. There was only one way to see if the pilot was still in the room. She reached into her pocket and pulled out a key.

Kelly's eyes flew open. She sat up with a start as the door banged against the latched chain. It wasn't a pleasant way to wake up but it wasn't uncommon. "No thank you. Not now." she said blearily. She knew it was just the maid but it still sent a shock of adrenaline through her system.

"Sorry. I come back later." The door clicked shut again.

"I'll be out in thirty minutes." Kelly responded. Rubbing her eyes, she reached over to turn the clock radio to face her. Eight am was a little early for housekeeping. There was no point in delaying getting up. She was awake. Swinging her legs off the bed and stretching in catlike luxury her thoughts turned to a hot shower and a good strong cup of Seattle's famous coffee. Last night's approach to the city had exhausted her.

Kelly combed fingers through her tousled hair and padded toward the bathroom thinking about today's trip to the museum. She smiled and turned on the shower. *It was going to be an interesting afternoon.*

In the hotel lobby Atta peered over the sports section of the newspaper and watched the maid as she held an animated conversation with Rasheed. His gaze shifted to another corner of the hotel where Wail sat. He didn't like the man. Wail reminded him of a frightened animal who had been kicked once too often. The anxious henchman looked into Atta's stare and immediately dropped his eyes. A watery smile flashed on and off as he struggled to find a safe place to look. Atta was disgusted. *One worked with what one was given.* He sighed and waited for Rasheed to finish his conversation.

The maid placed a key in Rasheed's hand and evaporated into the hallway. He stuffed it into his pocket and walked nonchalantly over to Atta.

"Do you have the business section?"

Atta handed him another piece of the paper. "Of course."

"Thank you. I want to check my stock in Delta Airlines." Rasheed replied, enjoying the irony of their coded chat. He sat down in a red Victorian chair next to his leader. "The pilot is just leaving her room. Should I go up now?" Before he could answer the elevator doors opened and Kelly stepped out. Atta didn't have to say anything. The minute Kelly went to the concierge desk Rasheed was in the elevator. Atta hid his expression behind the newspaper. Every time he looked at the woman he felt an uncontrollable rage rising. The fact that she was laughing and seemed to be enjoying her exchange with the silver-haired male concierge sickened him. *She was a perversion against Islam.* In his world a woman would be killed for being alone with an unauthorized man, much less speaking to him. All doubts about going forward with his plan were erased.

Kelly addressed her old friend fondly. "No thank you Henry. I don't need a taxi. The walk to the Taming of the Brew will do me good. I just wanted to make sure the Japanese exhibit was still at the museum."

"May I at least call a cab to pick you up from the Taming of the Brew?" the concierge asked.

"You spoil me Henry but I like it." Kelly grinned.

"You'll be going to the Seattle Asian Museum of Art then." he confirmed. Writing it down on a tablet. "I'll have a cab waiting for you outside the Taming of the Brew coffee shop in an hour."

Kelly picked up her raincoat and gave the older man a quick hug. "Thanks Henry. I'll see you later." The man reddened slightly, looked pleased and "harumphed" into his magnificent silver moustache.

Atta made a mental note of Kelly's itinerary. *Knowledge was power.*

The pilot slipped on her coat and headed out the door into a brisk wind and the cool mist of Seattle. Atta put his paper down and caught Wail gawking unabashedly after Kelly. Wail twitched, then froze, skewered on the intensity of the look he received from Atta. He wanted to be anywhere but here.

Upstairs Rasheed dug through the exterior pocket of Kelly's suitcase. He had looked everywhere else. Her Airline ID and pilot credentials were nowhere to be found. A uniform hung neatly in a corner but it would not fit any of them. It too was useless. *Mohammed will not be happy about this.* Rasheed worried. The zipper scratched his hand as he pulled out a fistful of stapled pages. He opened it, cursing as the end of a staple gouged his thumb. Sticking the wounded digit into his mouth he read the cover sheet. "Pilot Bid Package. First Officer Kelly Hunter. Employee number 172626. Rasheed slumped in relief, gave the suitcase another cursory swipe and hoped that the scant information would be enough to placate his now unpredictable leader. Atta's new plan was reckless. Unlike anything the wary Jihad leader would normally conceive. Rasheed had a bad feeling about it. He stuffed the papers into his shirt and exited the room as unobtrusively as possible.

Atta, Rasheed and Wail each left the lobby five minutes apart. They met several blocks away at their rented Ford Taurus. Atta opened the driver's side door and held out his hand.

"Give me the pilot's ID badge."

Rasheed dutifully pulled the package from his shirt and handed it to him.

"What is this?" Atta asked, his face darkening. Wail instinctively moved away from Rasheed.

"It is a pilot's bid sheet Mohammed." Something behind the look on Atta's face imploded.

Rasheed and Wail could see things crumbling behind the enigmatic expression. Watching their leader's cool methodical personality self-destruct was appallingly fascinating.

"Where are her pilot credentials and ID badge?" Atta demanded.

Rasheed consciously fought the urge to cower. "She must have them with her Mohammed. I searched the room and they weren't there." Rasheed waited for Atta's usual scathing reply and a return to the hotel for other less risky targets.

"Get in the car." Atta said. Rasheed and Wail looked at each other in disbelief.

"Where are we going Mohammed?" Wail asked. "To get the woman's badge and pilot credentials. Atta responded acidly. "Get in." Both men leapt to obey. They looked like two fish stunned by a stick of dynamite. An understanding of what they were about to do floated numbly to the surface. *Direct contact with a target was madness.* Rasheed and Wail barely had time to shut their doors before Atta keyed the ignition and sped off toward the Taming of the Brew.

Chapter Five
The Taming of The Brew

Feb. 20, 2001 / 09:54 am PST / Taming of the Brew coffee shop / Seattle, Washington.

"I'm not eccentric. I'm just more alive than most people."

- Dame Elizabeth Stillwell

Black-clad vampire wannabes flooded out of the coffee shop and passed ominously to Kelly's left. She smiled at them and they returned surprisingly innocent metal-studded grins. Light rain and downed tree branches were all that remained of last night's storm. Kelly tilted her face up to enjoy the feel of it on her skin. *Getting a glimpse of your own mortality did that to you.* she thought. *Life's small pleasures were magnified.*

Hanging over the door of her destination was a sign that announced "The Taming of the Brew" in old English script. She stepped off the rain-slicked sidewalk and drifted inside on a heady scent of Guatemalan coffee. The atmosphere was eclectic. A combination of Sherlock Holmes and Cosmopolitan chic. A familiar face beamed at her from behind the counter.

"Hey Kelly. Long time no see." Jeff's smile framed his stylish goatee. He was multi-tasking behind the polished wooden coffee bar. The brass espresso machine gurgled a welcome.

"I'm just glad to be here." Kelly replied. She clutched comically at her throat. "Need caffeine."

"Your usual?" The young man asked. It was a rhetorical question because he was already in the process of making it.

Kelly zeroed in on her favorite overstuffed chair. "I'm tempted to order something new just to throw you off." she laughed. "But why mess with perfection?" Dropping her raincoat on the armrest Kelly settled into the deep leather cushions. Smooth Jazz played in the background. Jeff hurried over with a large mug of latte and a cinnamon biscotti.

"I'll bet you had an interesting flight into Seattle last night." he smirked.

She smiled and shrugged. "Nah. Just sitting around doing nothing and letting the computers fly the airplane. You know how we are." He rolled his eyes. It was a private joke they shared. The young Barista aspired to be a commercial pilot and drank in every word. These visits from Kelly were an opiate to him.

"Yeah, right." he snorted. "I could hardly drive during that storm and you flew through it. The autopilot can't handle that kind of stuff. Tell me how you got in."

Kelly winked at him. "Later, kiddo. You've got a crowd waiting for you at the register." Chagrined, Jeff jumped up and made a beeline for the customers at the counter. Kelly lifted the steaming cup to her lips. She savored the first frothy sip, watching people drift inside from the rain. The heat from the mug thawed her chilled fingers.

Three men walked through the door. Two were tall and slim. The third was shorter and angular. There was a severity to this one's manner that preceded him like a silent shock wave. Kelly took a casual interest. The other men followed him with subdued resignation. One of them had a pockmarked face and a deer-in-the-headlights look that puzzled her. An aura of stress surrounded them all.

They look Middle Eastern. Kelly observed. *Probably foreign university students sweating mid-term exams.* Something about them made her want to scoot further back into her seat. The men looked directly at her. Then seemed startled to find her returning their stares. They all glanced away and pulled their chairs together at the back of the room, pointedly ignoring her.

Kelly focused her attention on the newspaper. It had been an odd encounter. She was used to men staring but this had been different. Almost threatening. Kelly chalked it up to a cultural thing and mentally moved on. Turning to the Arts section she verified the Japanese exhibit at the museum, looked at her watch and decided that it was time to go. Her past experience as a police aerial patrol surveillance pilot had instilled a healthy sense of paranoia. *Something wasn't right about the strangers at the back of the room.* The laid-back ambiance of the Taming of the Brew had lost its appeal.

Kelly finished her biscotti and swallowed the last of her latte. Jeff was still busy with the morning crowd of caffeine addicts. She left a generous tip on the plate and slipped out the door to meet her taxi.

Atta had deliberately seated himself with his back to the pilot. The electric blue of her eyes gave him the disturbing feeling that she could see right through him. Meeting that gaze had been a shock. *Women did not look a man in the eyes. It was considered an intimate gesture.* Atta adjusted his posture and watched her in the reflective glass of the Monet print on the wall.

"She's leaving." he stated, getting up as Kelly disappeared out the door. Rasheed and Wail stood too. Other than grabbing Kelly's purse if an opportunity presented itself they had no idea what they were supposed to do. They trailed toward the door behind their leader. Jeff looked up from handing his last customer their change and saw the men departing.

"Hey you guys. You forgot to pay for your coffees!"

Atta hesitated. The pilot was stepping into a taxi. He weighed the consequences of rushing out before he lost her and taking time to pay. The last thing he needed was an altercation with the clerk. Rasheed skidded to a stop and Wail collided with him. The commotion attracted the attention of the other patrons. They were watching to see how this would play out. Atta ground his teeth and shoved his hand in his pocket. He drew out a wad of American dollars.

"How much?" he demanded.

Jeff came from behind the counter wiping his hands on a towel. "What did you have? Was it a Venti Ethiopian coffee and two Grande Guatemalan Golds or was it the other way around?"

Atta glanced at the cab as Kelly shut the door. "It was the first." he hissed. "How much? We are in a hurry." The pressure was building in his head again. Jeff didn't like the man's attitude. He smiled and took his time. Kelly's cab pulled away from the curb in a spray of water.

"Let's see." Jeff murmured. "With tax that will be ten dollars and fifty-seven cents."

Atta stalked over to the counter and threw a twenty down. The pilot was gone but he knew where to find her. Jeff rang the bill up and handed Atta his change. The venomous look he got before the man hurried out the door was undeserved. Especially since they were the ones who tried to stiff him. He summoned up righteous indignation.

"Hey dudes!" he shouted. "What? No tip?"

The customers burst out laughing and went back to their coffees. Jeff grinned and shook his head.

Atta and his followers drove past the Seattle Asian Museum of Art. A rare glimpse of sunlight glittered on the Pacific Ocean giving the men a spectacular view from the hill. The splendor was lost on them. Only strategic positioning and finding their quarry mattered. They slowed in time to see the pilot disappear inside the impressive marble entry. Neither Wail nor Rasheed cared to ask Atta what he planned to do about it. The drive had been tense enough.

Time behind the wheel allowed Atta to reassess their situation and calm himself. Changing his mind was not in the cards, but he knew that he had been careless. He wondered if all great martyrs had been so driven as to lose themselves in their tasks. They drove around the block and parked on the opposite side of the tree-lined street.

"Watch the entrance. Phone me if she leaves." Atta instructed Wail. He opened his door and motioned Rasheed to accompany him. "We need to know how many exits the building has." Atta felt more in control of himself and everyone around him now.

"What are we doing Mohammed?" Rasheed asked uneasily, hurrying along in his wake.

Atta stopped and turned, nearly causing the larger man to trip over him.

"Must I paint you a picture? We are going to find the pilot and take what we need from her. Then we will leave." His words were deliberate, as if he were explaining the simplest of tasks to a slow child. Rasheed tried to hide his dismay.

"But Mohammed, we will draw attention to ourselves. The police." he objected.

"She is a woman alone. This is a country of criminals. It is easy. She is a soft target and the police will not care. We are doing the work of Allah, his name be praised." Atta gave his follower a look of utter disdain.

"Are you not a man?"

Rasheed was mortified. Of course Atta was right. "Yes Mohammed." he stammered. "I just wanted to know what was expected of me."

"To do as you are told." Atta answered him.

Chapter Six
Dark Angel

Feb. 20, 2001 / 10:55 am PST / Seattle
Asian Art Museum, Seattle, Washington

"A ship in harbor is safe - but that is not what ships are for."

- John A. Shedd

Kelly's footsteps echoed in the massive marble entry. A middle-aged woman behind the desk nodded a formal welcome. "May I help you?" The glasses perched on her nose gave her an owlish appearance.

"I'd like to see the Japanese cultural exhibit. How much is admission?"

The woman glanced around the empty reception area.

"Just one ticket? Are you by yourself?"

"Always." Kelly was surprised by her own answer. She hadn't realized how long she'd been alone, or that it even mattered. "Yes. Just one please."

"That will be five dollars." the woman stated. Kelly paid her and started toward a hall lined with ancient Samurai battle helmets. She wondered if it was time to take off her own emotional armor and immediately dismissed the thought with a shudder. Her two divorces had proven that a well-paid airline pilot tended to attract the wrong type of people for the wrong reasons.

Kelly's first marriage to another young bush pilot flying for the Selby Game Lodges in South Africa had been a happy one. Their pockets had been empty but their hearts had been full of love and adventures. Until Jake's untimely death left Kelly a young widow, pregnant with a baby son she adored as a final gift from him.

After being hired by her airline as their first female pilot years later, Kelly found herself and her paycheck relentlessly pursued by men who were nothing like Jake, but had been savvy enough con-artists to recognize what she wanted and present themselves as such until the vows were exchanged, the papers signed and they had complete access to her savings accounts and paychecks. Paychecks they'd spent on themselves and other women. Kelly had been happily single for four years now. Never telling strangers what she did for a living. Never dating. *I'm not going to mess up a good thing now.* She decided.

Shaking off the troubling thoughts, she raised her head and was captivated by what she saw. The room was dazzling, especially the display in the corner. Something in a large transparent case glowed with a warm golden light. She looked closer and was transfixed by the swirl of rich colors that flowed across the garment. Kelly all but put her nose against the glass. The object was extraordinary. One side of the short Kimono-style jacket was decorated with an intricate full-sized dragon. A blackened charcoal smudged surface on the inside obscured what was once a beautifully detailed picture of a tiger.

Kelly tilted her head for a better view, puzzled by the thickness of the material. *It's not silk. The material is at least three-eighths of an inch thick.* she thought.

"Leather fireman's coat. Edo. Circa 1600." The masculine voice next to her ear was tinged with humor. Kelly blinked, stood up and forgot to breathe. The coat was nothing compared to the extraordinary deep blue eyes that gazed into hers with such intensity.

"Sorry to startle you." he said. "I couldn't resist playing the scholar." He grinned and motioned over his shoulder. "I was wondering the same thing before I read about it on that plaque over there." He continued reading, deep in thought and equally entranced by the story he was narrating to her. "All of Japan's cities and temples were made of highly flammable wood and rice paper. Different fire companies were always in competition with each other for the glory of being the first ones on the scene to put the fire out. They held victory parades on the streets afterward and were celebrated as heroes when they did. The tiger side of this fire-fighting coat was worn on the outside when they were fighting the fires. The coat was reversed and the clean dragon symbol of this particular unit was displayed when they paraded through the streets in their victory marches."

Kelly couldn't think of a reply. The full sensual mouth smiled at her in amusement. His high cheekbones hinted at mixed ancestry. Shiny black hair tied into a short neat ponytail at the base of his neck completed the slightly exotic look. Kelly gathered her wits and smiled back at him.

Her cool words were at odds with the heat that flushed her cheeks. She offered the stranger her hand to shake.

"Well then professor." she said. "My name's Kelly Hunter. Where would a scholar recommend I go to find the Katanas in this exhibit?" He looked puzzled. "Japanese swords." she explained. "I collect them."

"Oh." he laughed. "I don't have a clue. I was hoping to find out where they display the Japanese bows. I'm an instinctive archer. Hardly a professor." He accepted her hand in a warm easy grip and shook it.

"Eugene Fletcher." he responded. "Call me Fletch or I won't know who you're talking to." A smile teased the corners of his mouth as he added "It's a pleasure to make your acquaintance - Kelly Hunter."

His hand was warm and strong. He seemed reluctant to release hers and stared at her in open admiration. She had difficulty looking away from those eyes. They spoke to her of things she missed and had tried to put out of her mind. She slid her hand out of his and changed the subject.

"The Japanese bow?" she said. "You must be a student of Kyujutsu."

He looked confused. Then his mouth twitched.

"Heck no ma'am. I don't even know how to spell whatever you just said. I'm just a Scottish–Comanche crossbreed cowboy who likes primitive and instinctive archery."

She nodded. "Then in a way you are a student of Kyujutsu." she assured him. "It's the art of mastering the bow. No bells and whistles like today's modern compounds, just pure archer and pure archery." Kelly grinned at him. He looked pleased.

"And you? he asked. "You don't actually use those Katanas do you?"

"Actually, I do." She struggled to keep a straight face. He looked both worried and intrigued. "Kendo." she explained. "Japanese sword fighting with full body armor."

Most men would have quailed at this news, made their excuses and beaten a hasty retreat. Fletcher's face blossomed into a full-blown feral grin. He looked absolutely delighted. "I had you pegged as more of a Viking Valkyrie than a Ninja warrior princess."

Kelly smiled. Both wary and intrigued, she was surprised to find she was rather enjoying the banter and the company of this man. She thought it was probably better to leave out the fact that she also had a first-degree black belt in Kempo karate. "Maybe I can claim to be a little bit of both then." she said. "Who says you can't have it all?"

Amused, he stopped himself short of saying "Can 1?" and wisely chose a safer topic. Huntsmen knew when to pursue and when to back off and he was good at what he did. It was his nature.

"Do you live here in Seattle?" he asked suddenly.

"No." she hedged. "I'm just here on business."

"So." he continued. "What sort of work do you do?"

Kelly drew on her standard answer. "I'm a heavy equipment operator." He looked skeptical. *The best defense is a good offense* she thought smugly. "What kind of work do you do?" she countered.

"I uh, work in human waste disposal." he smirked. Now Kelly looked skeptical. She gave him a raised eyebrow, and he responded with one of his own.

"You just never know who you'll meet wandering around a museum, do you?" she commented, dropping the subject.

"That's a fact ma'am." he agreed, letting his gaze flow over her. "You never know what kind of treasure you'll dig up either." This time Kelly knew she was blushing but she was safe. She would be leaving Seattle tonight and likely never cross his path again. *It's just a light-hearted bit of harmless fun they were both enjoying. No danger. No harm done. Why not enjoy today?*

Fletcher moved closer. This lady intrigued him. There was more to her than met the eye and what met the eye was beautiful. He decided that she was worth the wait.

"Well then Ms. Hunter, what say we team up on this museum expedition and go find those bows and Katanas?" His grin was infectious. She grinned back at him with equal enthusiasm,

"Lead on professor."

***

Outside Atta looked appraisingly at the man seated next to him. Wail picked nervously at his face and took an interest in the sparrows foraging outside the car. Rasheed was posted at the back of the museum in case the pilot chose to exit that way. Both men missed the distraction Rasheed's presence provided. Three hours alone in the car together was becoming intolerable. Atta was bored and angry at the delay.

"Wail."

The man jumped at his name and turned his attention from the birds.

"Yes Mohamed?"

"I have decided to reward you. You will be the one to take the woman's pilot credentials and badge from her when she leaves the museum." Atta was gratified to see Wail's eyes widen in alarm.

"But why am I deserving of this reward?" Wail asked apprehensively.

Atta folded his arms and closed his eyes, leaning his head against the seat back. "Because you have not questioned my decisions." He opened his eyes and added "and because you need the practice." The thought of the two people he detested the most being thrown at each other appealed to him. That, and Wail was expendable.

"But Mohamed, am I ready for this?"

Atta turned his head fixing his eyes on Wail. "Are you not ready to martyr yourself and slay a thousand infidels on the airplanes and in the buildings when the time comes Wail?" He brought his face closer. "Because if you're not ready to do that my brother, I will send you back to the Afghan training camps where they will make sure that you are."

Wail recoiled against the car door, wishing the pilot would come out or Rasheed would return. "I am ready. I will do as you say Mohammed." *A return to the camps was as good as a death sentence. Death with torture and dishonor. Then there was Wail's family. They would be punished too.*

"Of course you are." Atta said, leaning back and staring at the museum. "It is only taking paper from a woman. Even you can do that." he added.

***

Two hours later Fletcher and Kelly had found their bows and Katanas. They had also found a deeper understanding of themselves mirrored in each other. It all came so easily. The humor. The exploration. The curiosity and hunger for life and its challenges. It seemed natural to share confidences with each other that neither one of them had spoken of to anyone else. Kelly and Fletch stood together companionably gazing at a life-sized wooden carving of a great white owl. The feathers were shaped with such delicacy that it appeared a light wind could ruffle them.

Fletch studied it. Marveling at the wonder of a craftsman who could create such a beautiful thing. It brought back memories and a greater appreciation of his own mixed heritage. "The Snow Owl is my totem animal." he said. Fixing his eyes on the great bird. "My grandfather is a Shaman. He still lives on the reservation. He gave me my Comanche name." Kelly looked at him and felt she was being invited into a very private world. His eyes met hers. "My Comanche name is Hi'oopi Paraibo, Night Hunter.

That's what some Native Americans call the Owl." Fletch stared at it pensively. "It can be a good omen of wisdom and seeing through deception or a sign that death is near." He blinked and laughed self-consciously. "Sorry. I guess that sounds pretty-out there." he said.

Kelly held his gaze. "Not at all." she said, considering what she was about to say. "I do know that you don't share your Native American name with a stranger. It's a rare gift to someone you trust."

"Don't look so surprised." she smiled. "I may look Viking but I'm a mongrel of sorts too. One quarter Cherokee and Cheyenne. The Vikings got around. One of my friends is Cherokee. She gave me my name." Kelly hesitated. *She'd never shared it with anyone before. Why should she? It meant a great deal to her but few would understand or want too.* "My name is Wohale Unega un-oh-lee. Eagle in White Winds."

Fletcher was silent for a while. He felt their relationship shifting into something different. Something deeper. "Thank you." he whispered. Hesitating before saying "I liked sharing that with you." Something had changed. Kelly was suddenly aware of the heat of his body near hers but not touching. His breath smelled like rain. It ran across her skin like warm honey. He reached out and touched her cheek, his fingertips guiding her face up to meet his eyes.

Warnings shrieked through what we left of Kelly's conflicted brain. *This is dangerous. Not the fleeting safe flirtation she had expected but an attraction that could easily turn into passion, and more.* She found herself wanting more of it. Wanting him. Tears threatened and she cursed herself for a fool. She saw longing mixed with concern as Fletcher's winged brows drew together. The hunger in his eyes would have overwhelmed a lesser man.

"Kelly are you all right?" Fletch asked. She didn't want him to see the fear there. Pulling away from him was harder than she expected. It felt like she was tearing out a piece of her own flesh.

"I have to go." she said, catching her breath, "I'm about to miss my plane." He drew his hand back, a look of confusion crossing his face. It reached out and crushed her heart. *She had forgotten how painful it was to say no when you wanted to say yes.* "Today was wonderful." she said. "I have to go now." Her words begged forgiveness as she turned and ran for the exit. Fletch stood by the carving of the white owl wondering what had just happened. Watching her disappear around the corner, he felt an emptiness that hadn't been there before he'd met her. *That wasn't supposed to have happened.* he thought.

Kelly jogged down the steps of the museum entry and into the lowering fog of Seattle's late afternoon. She looked at her watch knowing that time wasn't what had driven her out. She was relieved at escaping an impending relationship and baffled at her simultaneous sense of loss. *Smooth move Kelly.* she admonished herself. *You finally find someone with possibilities after four years solo then you run away like Cinderella in track shoes. You really are a Basket case.* Stopping at the bottom of the stairs Kelly decided to take the alley at the side of the building. It led to a busy avenue where catching a cab would be easier.

Atta sat up in his seat. The pilot was finally coming out of the museum. He felt alive. The promise of violence always excited him.

"Wail be prepared. She's leaving." Wail obediently gripped the door handle, more than willing to get out of the car. Atta punched a number into the cell phone and brought it to his mouth. Rasheed answered immediately. "Ready yourself." Atta instructed. "The pilot is coming toward you in the alley. Do not let her pass."

"Yes, Mohamed." Rasheed said obediently. Atta hung up and turned to Wail. "The fog is in your favor. You know your task. Go." Wail didn't wait to be told again. He bailed out of the car and crossed the street as if the hounds of Hell pursued him. Atta got out and followed.

Chapter Seven
Predator and Prey

Feb. 20, 2001 / 2:12 pm PST / Seattle Asian Art Museum, Seattle, Washington

"All you are left with in a crisis is your conduct during it."

-   Johnnie Cochran

Kelly clutched the collar of her coat closer. Regret and relief both pushed at the edges of her attention. *It feels wrong to let someone inside your heart and push them out again.* she thought. Then she rationalized that it was better for them both this way. *Better now than later.* She hurried into the fog-wreathed alley distracted by her thoughts. Tendrils of mist lapped at her feet blurring her surroundings. A chill that was more than the cold mist of Seattle crept up her spine. *Something wasn't right.*

She stopped and raised her head. The hair prickled along the back of her neck. Peering into the darkening fog she saw him.

A figure framed against the far end of the alley. He was blocking the exit.

Kelly began to turn back the way she'd come in. She looked at the man again. Light from the setting sun glanced off his face. His swarthy features were vaguely familiar. Rasheed's eyes caught hers. Then they flicked nervously to the right, looking at something behind her. She glanced over her shoulder and saw the silhouette of another figure advancing hyena-like, through the murk.

This isn't happening. she told herself.

Running footsteps clattered behind her, destroying that flimsy hope. Kelly's right foot slid back. Her body automatically shifted into a solid fighting stance. Knees slightly bent, her hands moved into a defensive position. She calmed her racing mind. Using peripheral vision to keep both men in sight Kelly noticed that the figure at the head of the alley was also moving toward her at a slow walk.

This is real. she thought, taking a deep breath. The blood pounded in her ears.

You're going to have to handle both of these guys by yourself. She exhaled and the initial jolt of fear subsided. Her pulse slowed and her muscles relaxed. She sought the rhythm of her attackers. Kelly didn't think about winning or losing. She was only aware of the movement of the men. Prioritizing which one would arrive first. Then she let her well-trained body and muscle memory react. In her mind's eye the one closing the distance behind her appeared in slow-motion freeze-frame action. He would reach her in a matter of seconds.

Without thinking, her right leg shot back in a side thrust kick. The impact bent her attacker double as her foot hit its target. Air exploded from his lungs in a painful grunt. Kelly reversed her stance letting his inertia carry his chin into her elbow and his body over her well-placed leg. He went down onto his back with satisfying finality.

Shifting her feet, Kelly spun around to drive her knee into his chest. It wasn't necessary. His head hit the ground with a sickening thud that sounded like a melon dropped from a rooftop. She risked a quick look at him. His pockmarked face stared stupidly back at her. *He's one of the men from the coffee shop.* she realized with a shock.

Forcing herself to look up the alley she saw the first man rapidly closing the gap. Kelly's momentary distraction had cost her. He was running now and only ten feet away. This one didn't look dazed. He looked pissed.

Kelly shifted sideways to avoid his full impact. She could hear the first assailant on the ground moaning. *He would be on his feet again soon. This is bad.* she thought. *In fact, it couldn't get much worse.* Then she heard a third set of footsteps running behind her. Kelly moaned inwardly. *It just got worse.* Parrying a running punch that was aimed at her head she continued spinning and hooked the man's arm, using his momentum to guide him toward the sound of the footsteps behind her. She'd used this technique of fighting multiple opponents in her sparring matches. If she timed it right he should collide with the next assailant. She hoped it would buy her time to escape.

Kelly was breathing hard, knowing she'd hurt things that she'd feel later. If she was lucky enough to have a later. She released the man at the approaching runner. An outraged male howl accompanied the angry face of Fletcher as it shot out of a nimbus of fog. He caught her assailant in a head-on tackle. Both men hurtled past her in the opposite direction. They landed in a tangled heap of flailing limbs and muffled grunts as each struggled to gain control of the other.

The sick feeling that gripped her evaporated as she watched Fletcher vengefully bloodying her attacker. He had the man pinned to the ground beneath him using fists and elbows to batter his way past his opponent's defenses.

Evidently he knows how to take care of himself. Kelly thought with admiration. She turned to look for the pockmarked man. There was nothing left of him but a smear of blood on the dirty concrete and a swirl of fog left in his wake. Wail had gotten his wits about him. He'd taken a look at the situation and left his companion to fend for himself.

Kelly started toward the struggling men and stopped in mid-step. A clipped shout cut through the fog.

"Bas! Ma-be-Tash daram!" The disembodied voice bellowed a Farsi command from the darkness at the end of the alley. Everyone froze at the unexpected sound. The angular shadow faded in and out of the mist. Something sharp and deadly gleamed at his side in the last rays of the afternoon sun.

Kelly swallowed hard. She knew *You always get cut in a knife-fight. It was just a matter of where and how badly she'd get cut.* Fletch stopped and turned, his right fist poised for another strike.

"Let him up." the accented voice from the darkness instructed.

The bruised and bleeding man's hands had been raised to protect his face. He used the opportunity to shove Fletcher off him. The figure with the knife barked another command in what sounded like Dari and the injured man rolled to his feet, limping rapidly off into the fog.

Fletch was in a crouch, eyes riveted on the knife and looking for the bulge of an additional weapon. His hand rested almost casually on his knee. Kelly stayed where she was, listening for any sound indicating the return of the others.

"Throw your purse to me!" the figure flicked the blade in her direction. Adrenaline surged to anger as Kelly heard the demand. It seemed anticlimactic considering what they'd just been through.

"If that's all you want, why didn't you just say so?" she spat, pulling her wallet from her pocket. "How many jerks like you does it take to attack one woman anyway?"

The figure snarled something unintelligible and took a step toward her. It occurred to Kelly that now wasn't the time to be making him mad. His actions indicated that he would have preferred killing her to anything he might find in her wallet. He was holding back with a supreme effort of will.

"I don't think that's the way it's going down at all."

Kelly tore her eyes from the knife and looked at Fletcher. He was grinning and holding a Sig Saur p320 expertly in both hands. "Kelly. Would you stop glaring at the nice gentleman and step behind me? We don't want you smacking him with any hidden Katanas before he meets the police. He might file charges." Kelly slid warily behind him. She wondered where the gun had magically appeared from but was too relieved to care.

"Drop the knife and get down on the ground." Fletcher ordered.

The figure stood motionless in the billowing fog. His incorporeal voice sent three Dari words echoing down the alley. Kelly and Fletch tensed. *Something was about to happen.* The thing came hurtling at them from the other end of the alley. Clattering tin cans and screeching accompanied the writhing patch of fog. They both turned toward the sound as the spot blossomed into a ball of yowling fur and claws. It was not happy about being used as a distraction and makeshift piece of artillery. The old alley cat landed just short of them and scrabbled to its feet in a hissing mass of indignation. It looked at them balefully through slitted green eyes and sped off into the murk.

Kelly felt the tension release. She positioned herself behind Fletcher and he refocused his attention on where the man with the knife had been. Only fog and silence remained. They stood back-to-back, straining their eyes into the murky dusk.

"Are you all right?" Fletcher asked, never taking his eyes off the fog.

"I'm fine now that I remembered how to breathe again." Kelly answered. She noticed that her hands were shaking. She could hear her pulse pounding in her ears. Fletcher's warmth was a comforting reassurance against her back.

"Please tell me they're gone."

"I think you scared them off." he deadpanned. "Let's keep walking toward the main street."

Kelly let out a desperate-sounding giggle that frightened her more than what she'd just experienced. *She wondered if she was losing it or if Fletch was really that funny.*

"Where did you learn to fight like that?" he asked as they moved toward the glow of lights at the end of the alley. She suspected he was asking to take her mind off what just happened.

"Beating up kids and old people in Kenpo Karate for the last nineteen years." she said. "I teach in my spare time." Fletch made a sputtering sound and she could feel his shoulders shaking as he moved in sync with her. He appreciated a little black humor. "What are you doing packing heat?" she countered.

"Oh that?" he hesitated for a moment. "Big rats in the human waste disposal business. I have to um, get rid of them before they do too much damage to the… system."

"Must be really big rats." Kelly muttered to herself.

They moved out of the alley and into the welcome bustle of the city. Cars rushed by as a scattered group of people scurried happily past the storefronts and bistros. It was like breaking out of a nightmare and into a more innocent world. If not for their all too painful battle souvenirs the life and death events of the last few minutes might never have happened.

Fletch slipped his gun back into the hidden holster. He turned and looked at Kelly assessing the damage. Concern drew the skin tightly across his finely chiseled cheekbones.

Kelly looked at him and blurted out, "Who were those guys anyway? What the heck just happened?"

"I don't know." he said thoughtfully. "I need to tell you that what happened was not an aborted purse snatching. Those guys were too many, too organized and too controlled." He studied her, trying to reassure himself that she hadn't been badly injured.

"I think that they wanted something from you." he continued. "And it wasn't money. Have you ever seen them before?"

She felt a chill sweep her body that had nothing to do with the cold February

Seattle air or the fact that they were both soaked in fog and drizzle. Kelly knew he was right. "I'm pretty sure I saw the three of them together at the coffee shop I was at this morning but that was in town." she replied. "What are they doing way out here?"

Fletch looked at her and smoothed back stray strands of his hair with both hands. The gesture bought him time to think of the best way to pose the question. "Kelly, you and I both know they showed up here because they were looking specifically for you. Is there something you're not telling me? Are you in some kind of trouble?" His voice was heavy with concern.

Kelly felt the frustration building inside her. *He thinks I had something to do with this.* she realized. Her throat had a lump in it and the impending threat of tears made her angry with herself. Kindness and concern did that to her. It tore down the walls. She felt vulnerable. "I've told you everything I know." she protested. "I'm not in some kind of trouble and none of this makes any sense to me!" She immediately regretted her tone of voice.

"I'm sorry." she whispered. Her body was having a delayed reaction and beginning to shake in the aftermath. "This whole day has had a surreal aspect to it. I'm still a bit dazed." Kelly admitted. "I didn't mean to take it out on you."

Fletch smiled and moved closer, taking her hand and pulling her to him. "It's ok to drop the katana now Kelly." he said. "You're with a friend." He wrapped his arms around her and she relaxed into his embrace, resting her head against his shoulder. To the casual observer they were just another happy couple on the sidewalk.

Had it really been this good to let someone she could trust take over? Kelly wondered. Her pain and her fear evaporated into the warmth of his body. He held her until the shaking stopped.

"You really need to file a police report on this." Fletch said, turning his face into her hair. He waited for a response and added "Please… I'm worried about you."

"I will." she sighed, enjoying the moment. "I don't live here. Whoever they were they won't find me again." She felt strangely calm and better than she could remember feeling in a long time.

A horn startled them out of their moment and a taxi hydroplaned to a stop at the curb. Frazzled red hair covered the balding head that hung out the window. An equally red nose bobbed above the indignant mouth.

"Lady I've been circling the block for thirty minutes looking for you. I turned down some good fares in the process. Either get in now or I'm leaving without you." Kelly recognized the driver who'd dropped her off.

"I am so sorry," she began.

"The lady was just attacked back there in the alley." Fletcher cut in. "Give her a minute." The cabby's tone switched from combative to begrudging concern.

"If I were you mister, I'd put her in this cab. She told me to come back and pick her up again thirty minutes ago. She's got a flight to catch. We'll decide on the way if she wants to go to the hospital, the police station or her hotel." Other horns honked impatiently behind him.

"I'm blocking traffic." he said anxiously.

Kelly gave Fletch a quick hug and got in the cab. She rolled down the window in time to say "thank you." The rest of her words were lost as her cab sped off into the traffic and Seattle's evening drizzle. Fletch dodged the curtain of dirty water thrown up in their wake. He brushed the moisture from his soaked jeans and cursed himself for not getting her phone number.

Chapter Eight
Aliases

Feb. 21, 2001 / 07:30 am PST / Mayflower Hotel Seattle, Washington

"If you want to see God laugh, plan your life.

- Yiddish Proverb

The alarm went off. Adding insult to injury, the phone rang at the same time.

Kelly's hand swatted at the offending sounds, hit the snooze button on the clock and fumbled for the phone. Clutching at the receiver she brought it to her ear and was greeted by a cheery "Good morning. This is your wake-up call."

"Thank you." she mumbled blearily. Then she woke up enough to realize she was talking to a recording. Kelly levered herself into a sitting position and replaced the receiver. Henry had given her a message from Captain Granger last night. Mercifully, their flight had been cancelled. The same storm that hit them in Seattle had turned into a blizzard of Biblical proportions and closed down the airport in Salt Lake City. They were flying out this morning instead.

She winced. Her right elbow felt like it had been hit with a baseball bat. Kelly opened her eyes and inspected it. There was a throbbing purple lump the size of a hen's egg just below her elbow. Twisting to inspect her arm brought a twinge of pain to her lower back. She took great satisfaction in knowing her attackers were probably waking up with more memorable souvenirs than she had.

A quick shower washed away some of the aches and revealed a variety of colorful scrapes, bumps and bruises she hadn't noticed before.

Toweling off, she turned on the weather channel while she dressed and packed. The screen showed a line of snow showers passing over the Rocky Mountains. *Denver's in for it.* she thought. *Salt Lake should have nothing worse than a blanket of snow and plowed runways now.*

Kelly finished putting her uniform on and ran a brush through her hair. She took one last look in the mirror and adjusted the brim of her hat before heading down to the front desk. Glancing at her watch she was happy to see that it was only eight-thirty. *Plenty of time to check out and enjoy a chat and cup of coffee with Henry.*

The doors of the elevator slid open to reveal the opulent lobby. Henry approached with a silver tray bearing a coffee pot, two China cups, milk and sugar. Kelly tossed her key behind the vacant desk and headed for the cozy Victorian sitting area.

Henry slid into the armchair next to her and poured them both their traditional cups of coffee. Then he settled down to enjoy a chat and hearing what she'd been up to. By the time he finally took a sip of his own coffee it was cold.

Kelly finished her story and the last drops of her own cup. Henry stroked his moustache and shook his head. "I'm probably just paranoid." she added. "But I think someone's been through my suitcase. I can't find my pilot bid package anywhere and the zipper on the pocket was open."

"If it were anyone but you, I wouldn't have believed it." Henry said. "Be careful out there. I'm going to do some checking with hotel security while I'm at it." he said thoughtfully. "What happened to you concerns me."

"Thanks Henry." Kelly replied. "It worries me too." Henry picked up Kelly's bags and took them out the door to the crew van.

A chime sounded and the elevator doors opened. Captain Granger stepped out looking considerably more rested than the last time she'd seen him.

"Good morning, Bill." Kelly greeted him. "Did you have a good layover?"

Bill put his flight kit down beside his suitcase and handed the room key to the sleepy clerk behind the desk. " "Morning Kelly. Yes I did. I must have slept half the day, worked out, bid for my next month's flight schedule and did my taxes. You know. The normal layover stuff." He took the receipt from the desk clerk.

"I just had room service." he told the clerk. Bill signed for the charges and looked up. "I see you got my message about our flight cancellation since you didn't leave without me last night. How about you? All rested up?"

"Rested and ready." she smiled. "I got my workout too." They threw their raincoats over their arms and walked to the crew van waiting outside. The air was moist and bracing. The sun was still shrouded in Seattle's early morning mist.

"I didn't see you in the workout room." Bill said, climbing into the van. "When did you go down?"

Kelly shrugged. "I didn't. I did a little Karate." The van driver slid the door shut and climbed in as they fastened their seatbelts.

"Do you think that martial arts stuff would work in a real fight?" Bill asked. The van pulled out into the Seattle morning traffic.

"I guess you never know until it happens." Kelly responded. "It can't hurt."

She didn't feel like discussing what happened. Too many unanswered questions. It was all too bizarre. She barely believed it herself. The rest of the ride passed in companionable silence.

Passengers were sitting in the waiting area when Kelly got to the gate. She walked to the podium and smiled at the svelte agent behind the desk. He glanced back at her and his eyes crinkled in welcome. "Well, if it isn't my favorite pilot. I heard you were delayed going through airport security. The captain picked up the flight plan and the rest of the crew is on board." He motioned a passenger to the front of the line. "Good to see you Kelly."

"Thanks Ken. You too." She was impressed with the good-natured professionalism of gate agents in general. Ken was unflappable. Even in the worst of circumstances.

Kelly set her bags down by the jetway door, punched in the code, scanned her ID badge and went inside. The shrill whine of jet engines assailed her ears. A familiar odor of jet fumes seeped down the chilly jetway as she walked toward the open door of the aircraft. *I love the smell of jet fuel in the morning.* Kelly thought. She always had. Ever since she was a hopeful aviation obsessed little girl at her first air-show.

"Hey Kelly. How goes it girl?" A smiling ebony face framed in a neat fashionable afro peered around the doorway. Shaheera was one of the most beautiful ladies Kelly had ever seen, and her best friend. The rest of the flight attendants were busily checking and securing the cabin and galleys.

"Excellent O' Nubian Princess." Kelly pulled her suitcase over the threshold and unhooked her flight case to put it in the cockpit. "How have you been?"

Shaheera's face lit up and Kelly was rewarded with a luminous smile. "I've been good." Shaheera said. Then she grinned mischievously. "Well, maybe a little bad but my boyfriend says that's a good thing too." She put her fingers to her lips and widened her eyes.

"Oooh, did I say that?"

Kelly laughed at her friend's audacity.

"Coffee?" Shaheera offered.

"No thanks. I'm already on caffeine overload." Kelly declined. "Water would be great."

Kelly slipped her raincoat on and turned to go outside to begin a check of the aircraft. She would program the flight route, speeds, and weights for the captain when she got back to the cockpit.

Shaheera gave her a thumbs-up. "You got it girl." and went back in the galley, humming happily.

The security door slammed shut behind Kelley as she trotted down the steep metal stairs to do her pre-flight inspection. Sliding her gloved hand down the wet steel railing, her eyes automatically traced the lines of the black bullet-shaped nose looming over her.

Kelly shone her flashlight over the surface. She moved methodically around the 757 closely inspecting all wheel wells, surfaces and moving parts within the reach of her flashlight beam.

Moisture dripped from the brim of her hat when she climbed back up the corrugated metal stairs. Giving the top of the wings and fuselage one last check at the doors, she punched the code on the jetway door's lock and walked back into the warmth of the cockpit.

Bill was comfortably ensconced in the captain's seat, rolling his Styrofoam cup of hot coffee lazily between his hands, enjoying the heat. Kelly hung her wet raincoat up in the closet and clipped her hat to the wall. Pegging her uniform jacket on a separate hanger, she climbed over the control pedestal into her chair.

"You looked like you might be detained back in security for a while so I programmed the flight for you. Want to check my work?" Bill asked. Kelly looked at him gratefully.

"Thanks Captain Granger." Kelly deliberately used the honorific title. "Like I said. I'll follow you anywhere." She bent to run through the programming of the Flight Management System. Bill looked pleased with himself.

Ken's smooth gate agent voice reverberated in the cockpit followed by his well-groomed head of hair. "I hate to interrupt this Kodak moment captain, but we have a couple of armed Federal Law Enforcement Officers coming aboard. I thought you might want to meet them before I board the passengers." Ken handed the confidential seating data to the captain.

"Absolutely Ken." Bill replied, taking the two boarding pass copies. "Bring them on up to the cockpit."

Kelly finished checking the flight plan and started reviewing her departure plates. "I'll be ready to do the checklist in just a minute Bill." she said, setting a departure frequency on the radio."

Shuffling feet announced the presence of someone at the cockpit door.

"Captain Granger," Ken announced, "these are the two Federal Air Marshals I was telling you about. They're armed and will be going to Salt Lake City with you. Then on to Washington, DC."

Kelly turned in her seat and looked up into two riveting blue eyes. They were looking back at her with the same startled bewilderment and pleasure. The finely crafted brows raised in surprise. Kelly forgot to breathe.

"Haven't you ever seen a female airline pilot before Agent Fletcher?" Ken laughed. "This is First Officer Kelly Hunter." He noticed the stunned silence and explained, "She has that effect on lots of people."

Kelly's face grew hot.

"Close your mouth Kelly." Captain Granger instructed. "Haven't you ever seen a Federal Air Marshall before?" She hadn't realized that her mouth was open. Kelly snapped it shut and took a deep breath. She extended her hand and introduced herself.

"First Officer Kelly Hunter." she said. "I don't think that I've ever met a Federal Air Marshall either but I do believe that I've met a human waste engineer who specializes in big rats." She tried to maintain the professional façade, looking seriously into his eyes.

"Agent Eugene Fletcher." he responded, struggling with the corners of his mouth. He took her hand and shook it. "It's a pleasure to meet you ma'am."

"I don't believe I've ever met a real honest-to-God Lady airline pilot either." he hesitated. "Unless you'd categorize the job description as a heavy equipment operator." Fletch looked around. "What does this thing weigh anyway?" Captain Granger, the gate agent and Fletcher's partner all looked at each other in puzzlement. "About three hundred thousand pounds." Kelley stated. "Give or take a few." She was pleased that her voice stayed level and sounded matter-of-fact.

Fletch didn't let go of her hand. He turned it so he could see her arm more clearly. "That's one heck of a colorful bruise and goose egg of a bump you have there. Lifting this whole thing all by yourself, are you?"

Kelly pulled his hand closer to her face. She inspected his swollen black and purple knuckles. "Hmm." she smirked. "Don't you guys use guns on the bad people or do you just beat them into submission?"

Fletch grinned. "The job's easy." he stated looking into her eyes. "It's the layovers that'll get you." They both laughed.

"Ah, if you two are through here I'm Captain Bill Granger. It's a pleasure to have you on board."

Fletch released Kelly and shook Bill's hand. His demeanor immediately became all business. "Eugene Fletcher, and this is my partner, Carl Smith."

The bewildered Smith looked between Kelly and Fletch and shook Bill's hand. "Pleased to meet you, Captain." Carl said. He looked at Kelly and hesitated.

"Don't be afraid Carl." Fletch chuckled, dragging his partner closer. "She doesn't bite." Fletch looked thoughtful. "At least I don't think she does."

The gate agent chimed in "She has that effect on lots of people." he said reassuringly. Kelly rolled her eyes and shook Carl's hand.

"Kelly Hunter. It's nice to meet you Carl." He looked relieved.

"We'll be in seats 2A and 3B if you need us," Fletch informed them.

"Thank you, gentlemen." Kelly said. "We'd better get back to work now."

"Same here." Fletch agreed holding Kelly's gaze for one more moment. Then he turned and left taking Carl and a bemused Ken with him.

Bill turned and eyed Kelly suspiciously. "What was that all about?" he asked.

"What?" Kelly widened her eyes. "Haven't you heard? I have that effect on lots of people."

Chapter Nine
Atta

Feb. 21, 2001 / 09:11am PST / Mayflower Hotel / Seattle, Washington

"To be properly wicked you do not have to break the law, just follow it to the letter."

-   Anthony De Mello

Atta slammed his fist down on the cheap hotel desk. Kelly's bid package fell and landed on the stained carpet. Wail jumped at the gesture, sweat filming his sallow features. Across the room Rasheed stood slumped against the wall. His arms were crossed protectively over his chest. He peered at the scene through the collage of bandages swathing his bruised features.

"A simple task!" Atta snarled turning to face them. He poised himself over the cowering man with the pockmarked face. "I give you one simple task Wail. To get the woman's pilot certificates and security badge so that we can track her. You cannot even take something from a soft target, a woman, without failing and calling attention to us!" he hissed grabbing Wail by the hair and dragging him to the floor.

Wail stifled a scream, tears running down his ravaged face. He clutched at Atta's hand as he was dragged to his knees. He had never known Atta to lose control or do anything like this. *What is happening?* he wondered in alarm.

"Allah, razi kardan, please!" he begged. "Forgive me Mohammed!" Atta jerked Wail's head back and stared into his panicked eyes. What Wail saw there was worse than his fear of Atta's anger. The flat black pupils had expanded to fill the whole of the iris and there was an expression in them that was a strange mixture of violence and pleasure. *I should have killed the woman, Kelly Hunter, in the alley and been done with it!* He thought. That was where his real rage was coming from. It had been humiliating.

Atta looked at him for a moment. Then the shutters closed and the eyes went dead again. Their blackness stood out against Atta's bloodless skin. Wail froze. Atta loosened his grip on Wail's hair and heaved a shuddering sigh. Rasheed stayed in his place against the wall, one eye swollen shut and the other wide open. Atta stood over his crouching victim. He hated losing control and he had done it twice in the last twenty-four hours. *Succumbing to emotion means compromising the mission.* he reminded himself. *It is a weakness.* Atta rubbed a hand over his face wondering what was wrong with him. Until a few days ago he'd easily been able to present himself as polite and chatty with most of the infidels and all of his Jihadis when it suited his purpose. *No matter now.* he decided. *It was almost over. If he could just keep everything together and under control for a few more months. If this was what it took so be it.*

That was what he hated most in the weak and groveling Wail. What he had hated most in himself as a child. His stepfather had beaten him and called him "madar pesar, a mama's boy." and he had cowered. The euphoric rush that Atta experienced every time he gave in to violence, domination and the power it gave him over another was too distracting. He forced himself to step back and steady his voice.

"Stand up." he said, offering his hand. Wail took it warily and stood up in a submissive posture. Atta studied him speculatively for a long moment. "It may be that you have been made incompetent by the soft living and temptations that we are forced to adopt in this infidel culture," Atta suggested. Wail looked alarmed and started to protest.

Holding up his finger in a silencing gesture Atta continued. "It is not your fault my brother. We are subjected to many stresses in undertaking this holy Jihad." The slumping Wail looked up and chanced a hopeful smile.

"I will arrange for you to be extracted to Afghanistan for Rest and Relaxation and an opportunity to restore yourself to a true warrior's capabilities." Wail uttered a small desperate whimper. It was met by a stony look from his leader. A glance at Rasheed found no sympathy there either. Rasheed had wisely dropped his eyes.

Atta's decision was akin to a death sentence for Wail and they all knew it. Al Qaeda operatives in cells inside the United States were selected for their basic language skills and loyalty to the Jihad. To be sent back to Afghanistan for R&R meant that they were under suspicion of being a rogue agent or corrupted and a danger to the mission. The best that Wail could hope for now was to somehow prove himself under the brutal scrutiny of the Al Qaeda training camps.

Atta turned to Rasheed dismissing the distraught Wail as if he were a piece of furniture. "Our mission to place the explosive device on the United Airlines flight tonight has been cancelled." Atta stated. It was hard to tell if Rasheed looked relieved or disappointed beneath the bandages. Atta continued. "Our controller has decided that the mission was compromised because of Wail's incompetence with the woman and the man with the gun."

Wail cringed guiltily. He could feel the men's contempt settling over him. Neither one gave him a second glance. *But the woman had unforeseen skills in fighting!* Rasheed wanted to shout. *I did not fail you!* It didn't occur to Wail that Atta's insistence on the confrontation in the alley might have been the problem.

Atta had never intended for them to plant a bomb aboard the flight. This was just one of the methods he used to test the men's trustworthiness and the security of his cell. He often gave Wail and Rasheed false instructions about operations like this. The only ones who were aware of the ruse were Atta and higher ups like Bin Laden.

If security was stepped up on the flight in question or a bomb threat phoned in Atta knew that one of his men had turned or that his line of communication had been breached by U.S. intelligence. In this case everything appeared secure.

Atta savored Wail's pain and Rasheed's fear of failure. *It is a good reminder of the consequences of disappointing me.* he thought. His two subordinates waited stoically for his instructions.

A sense of satisfaction warmed Atta as he pictured the confusion that so many false threats had caused the CIA and American intelligence. *The more we cry wolf the less likely they are to take the real threat seriously when our time comes.*

"Tonight we leave on the United Airlines Flight to Florida." He stated. "We will be watching cockpit entry and exit patterns and looking for security weaknesses on this flight." Atta didn't tell either man that they would be parting ways. He'd already made the arrangements. His face showed nothing as he contemplated his plans. *Wail would be escorted back to Afghanistan by other Al Qaeda operatives. He and Rasheed would go back to Florida where Atta would continue his pilot training.* The terrorist leader congratulated himself on keeping his men psychologically off balance. They were never certain of his plans. This kept him in complete control and his decisions unchallenged. *They don't even trust each other.* Atta thought. *All that they have is the Jihad and their fear of me.* His smile painted a tight thin line across his lips.

"Pack everything and sanitize the area today." Atta instructed. "We will not be returning." He turned his head slightly and glanced at them both. They stood as if uncertain whether they were allowed to move yet or not.

"Now." He stated flatly.

Overcast late afternoon drizzle washed the windshield as Atta backed their rental car out of the Holiday Inn parking lot. Rasheed sat in the passenger seat and recalled his quick goodbye to Wail. They had checked out shortly after observing prayers in their room. As they walked to the parking lot a white Dodge Intrepid pulled into the parking space next to them. Atta walked to the window of the Dodge and spoke briefly to the man inside. Then he told Wail to get in the Intrepid.

The thin frame of Rasheed's friend had slumped in dejection as he turned a puzzled face toward them. Atta seemed to be enjoying himself as he smiled and said "They are taking you to the airport Wail." He offered no further explanation, leaving it to

Wail's anguished imagination to determine whether he would be joining them again or going on a much longer journey.

Rasheed had barely managed to say "Inshallah, God be with you" to Wail as he watched the man's ashen face peering out the back window. The Dodge turned the corner and disappeared onto the main highway.

He felt more than saw Atta staring at him in displeasure. Rasheed turned. He was almost afraid to look knowing that his small display of humanity in saying goodbye had been a mistake.

"Use English in public Rasheed." Atta directed. "Have you too forgotten we are on a mission and that our cover must not be broken?"

"No Mohamed. Thank you for reminding me." he said. "I apologize." To his relief this seemed to mollify Atta. Rasheed knew better than to plead excuses or argue with his unpredictable leader. He also knew better than to ask if they would ever see Wail again.

Atta was in a jovial mood as he turned the wheel and headed toward Seattle Tacoma International Airport. He had reason to be. When Atta had finally taken the time to look, he'd discovered that Rasheed had accidentally stumbled onto a wealth of information when he grabbed Kelly Hunter's pilot bid package. The papers contained a code and phone method of tracking her flight schedule indefinitely. It was perfect. The pilot ID and credentials would have been virtually useless in comparison. The excuse to replace Wail had been an added benefit. Atta entered the freeway and turned his thoughts to the business at hand. He recited their pre-planned cover story. "We will be in seats 2B and 3C first Class." he said as they accelerated. "Your injuries are the result of an auto accident in a taxi cab. We were hit from behind but apart from some minor cuts and bruises everyone is fine." Atta slid over to the fast lane.

Rasheed listened intently. *It was ironic how much Atta was willing to risk by speeding and still driving without a valid driver's license in spite of his anal attitude toward keeping a low profile. Atta had already been stopped once for speeding without a current driver's license and received a ticket for it. It had gone unpaid.* "Yes Mohamed." he responded. "I understand."

"Good." Atta said. "You will also keep silent as much as possible. I will speak for us. If offered alcohol accept it." Atta frowned. "We must put aside Islamic practices to blend in for the greater purpose of Jihad." he continued. "We are engineering students here to study for our pilot's licenses at the Huffman Aviation Flight School in Venice, Florida."

Rasheed nodded. "Yes Mohamed." He accepted whatever fate Allah chose for him and relaxed enough to enjoy the scenery as they sped past a van with the Mayflower Hotel logo on it. His mind was vaguely aware of uniformed crew members riding in it. Then it was gone.

Rasheed chanced a nervous glance at his self-satisfied leader and mentally questioned what he didn't dare put into words. *Why has Atta taken such a risk by stalking the female for her credentials when we were trained never to call attention to ourselves? What is wrong with him?* Rasheed wondered again.

He decided not to dwell on his leader's mood swings between driven rigidity and flagrant risk. It was easier to trust in Allah and do what he was told than to worry about it. He shook himself free of such traitorous thoughts.

Atta's attention was drawn to the small movement. Do you need a painkiller Rasheed?" he asked. "Your injuries do not seem that bad."

"No Mohamed." Rasheed assured him. "It is only this infernal cold wet weather. I will be fine." Rasheed secretly gave thanks for the Fatwa that gave him permission to drink alcohol on the flight. They pulled into the Avis parking lot and took the bus to United's curb-side check-in. The driver walked to the back and pulled their luggage out of the trunk.

"Is that all of it sir?" the driver asked.

"Yes." Atta said, skipping the tip.

The men checked two bags at the curbside. The luggage contained some fireworks and certain electrical components that could be construed as an explosive device if they were assembled. A Swiss army knife and an unloaded gun were also packed. These were not illegal when shipped in the cargo hold but Al Qaeda was always testing the system. If these items were undisturbed they were undetected. Atta was particularly curious about the gunpowder contained in the fireworks. C4 explosives were more to his liking but that would have been too obvious.

"United." Atta stated, handing the bags to the Skycap. They were placed on a trolley and wheeled away. Atta turned and strode through the terminal doors with Rasheed trailing him. Airport Security and the boarding gates were to their right. They turned and headed off down the shop-lined concourse. A faint aroma of coffee, toast and bacon wafted through sleepy morning crowds as the airport came to life. The soft murmur of people greeting and saying goodbye to loved ones was jarred by repetitive loud recordings urging them to guard their luggage and not park in the loading zones.

Atta and Rasheed found the shortest of the long lines through security and set their other two carry-ons down. These contained a boxcutter, a Gerber multi-tool and a sharpened credit card. Atta engaged an older couple behind them in a pleasant conversation involving the weather and Rasheed's unfortunate auto accident. Rasheed just smiled and nodded an aggrieved thank you to their expressions of concern and sympathy. The line moved sluggishly ahead.

Ten minutes later they were smiling at the Security Agent and dutifully placing their bags on the conveyor belt for screening.

Chapter Ten
Wings

*Feb. 21, 2001 / 10:56 am MST / DAL #1224
enroute SEA/TAC to Salt Lake City, Utah*

"Dad, I left my heart up there."

- **Francis Gary Powers,**
CIA U-2 pilot shot down over the
Soviet Union, describing his first
flight at age 14.

The raptor-like silhouette of the 757 left a thin white contrail across the sky as it winged its way East. Viewed from the ground it was hard to imagine hundreds of people sitting peacefully in such a tiny silent speck. The sun caught the silver underbelly as it banked, causing it to flash like a diamond.

Delta Flight 1224 had departed Seattle on schedule and climbed like a homesick angel in the cool crisp air. Kelly was enjoying the duties of the "Pilot Not Flying" while Captain Granger took his turn at the yoke. The deep greens and blues of

Seattle slid below them. Mount Rainer towered majestically in the distance.

Kelly completed the climb checklist and switched her microphone to the Passenger address system. "Ladies and Gentlemen." she began. "On behalf of Captain Bill Granger, myself and our cabin flight crew we would like to welcome you aboard Delta Airlines Flight 1224 to Salt Lake City."

She twisted to look out her side window. "Off to the right" she said "you can see Mount Hood, the tallest Mountain in Oregon." Kelly unfastened her shoulder harnesses and settled herself more comfortably in her seat as she continued. "If you look beyond it you will see the remnants of Mount St. Helens still smoldering in the distance." She added a brief history of the Mt. St. Helens eruption and moved on to the estimated time of arrival in Salt Lake City and the weather conditions there.

Sitting comfortably in first class Fletcher found himself caught up in listening to Kelly's voice. With each syllable came images of Kelly talking conspiratorially with him in the museum, her eyes sparkling with laughter.

He could still feel himself standing quietly with her, their arms barely touching and their body heat captured in the small space between them. He remembered watching so many emotions flow across her face. Mischievousness, delight, passion, desire and pain had all danced there. Then he thought of Kelly alone in the fog in the alley fighting for her life. His jaw clenched at the thought. He could almost feel the soft silkiness of her hair against his cheek as he held her to comfort her and the light fragrance along the warmth of her neck that was uniquely hers. *If you could smell sunlight on the wind,* he thought *that would be her scent.*

"Would you like a refill on that sir?" a voice next to his ear asked. Fletcher's hand bumped the half-full coffee mug but he managed to steady it before it spilled. He looked up into the smiling ebony face of Shaheera and silently cursed himself for letting his mind wander and being caught off guard.

Daydreaming about the pilot is a good way to get us all killed. he told himself harshly. *Pay attention to your surroundings.* "Coffee with milk and a touch of sweet and low please." Shaheera hurried off with the request and Fletch slunk down in his seat determined not to let that happen again.

An hour later they began their gradual descent out of 38,000 feet. The glittering white diorama of Salt Lake City and the towering Wasatch Mountains spread out ahead of them. North of the City, the Great Salt Lake was rimmed with snow.

Kelly was harassing Bill by inquiring if he needed any help making the approach under these difficult conditions. He responded in kind with a critique of her heavy-handed flight control technique on her last approach into Seattle.

"No thanks." Bill declined. "I don't think I should subject any more passengers to the wild gyrations that you put them through on the last flight." He laughed. "Any pilot can land in a hurricane and make it look good. It takes a real pilot to make an impression in smooth air."

"You've got that right." Kelly agreed. "No excuses for a bad landing on this one." Captain Granger snorted derisively and turned his attention back to the flight instruments, but they were both grinning.

Kelly had been feeling unusually happy since Fletch came on board. She liked knowing he was only a few feet behind the cockpit in the first-class section. *A human waste engineer indeed.* she thought. *There's no way someone can move like that and not be a trained fighter.*

Kelly looked at the altimeter and noted that they had another ten thousand feet to go before she needed to read the descent checklist. She drifted, remembering Fletcher's eyes and the first look that had passed between them. *Definitely desire there.* she thought. *but something more than that.* Kelly had only seen that kind of fire in the eyes of someone who had chosen the way of the warrior. He had acknowledged her as a kindred spirit. She found herself wanting to know what it would feel like to wrap herself around him and fill this vast numbed emptiness that had been her heart with his kind of passion.

"Descent check please." The voice of Captain Granger cut through her reverie. Kelly looked up to find the altimeter winding down through 18,000 feet. The altitude where the altimeters were set to the field elevation and the descent checklist was read.

"Altimeters?" she responded, embarrassed that she'd almost missed it.

"What's the current field setting in Salt Lake?" Bill asked.

"Two niner eight five." Kelly responded, checking the weather and adjusting her own altimeter.

Stop that! she scolded herself. *You're an airline pilot and you almost missed setting your altimeter because you're daydreaming about the FAM back there like some schoolgirl with a crush.* Shocked at her lapse of professionalism, Kelly forced her thoughts of Fletch to the back of her mind and resumed the checklist. She was usually good at compartmentalizing her thinking when flying and putting distracting thoughts in a box to be opened at a later and more appropriate time.

"Do you think you can handle a good one for a change?" Bill asked, rolling the big aircraft to the left as the airport came in sight.

"What?" Kelly startled, looking at him as if he could read her mind.

"I said do you think that you can handle the idea of me making a good landing for a change? Because I'm going to grease this one on unless you make bad altitude call-outs. In that case a bad landing will be your fault and not mine."

"I'll be talking you all the way down so any good landing will be my doing because you were only following orders." Bill gave her a defiant look and applied his attention to the runway ahead as he rolled out on final approach.

"Roger Salt Lake. Delta 1224 is cleared to land on runway 16 Right." Kelly acknowledged the landing clearance and turned her attention to the radar altimeter. She wanted Captain Granger's landing to be a good one for him.

"One thousand feet above touchdown and cleared to land." she said. "Looking great Bill. You've got it wired. Steady sink rate and the airspeed is right on." She smiled approvingly at his focused concentration and knew that he would like the results. After his previous decision not to divert from Seattle he needed the confidence builder. Pilots had no depth perception before 50 feet above touchdown. Then they had to look a long way down the runway for it to be effective.

The big jet worked its way down to the twelve-thousand-foot runway and gingerly stopped its descent within a foot of it. The left main gear poked tentatively at the asphalt and touched down. The right main followed and the nose wheel gently lowered to the runway. Captain Granger pulled the throttles to idle and smoothly applied reverse thrust. "Man, I give good callouts!" Kelly announced as they taxied off the runway.

Bill tried to look nonchalant as he called for the after-landing check and headed for the gate. "Thank you I think." he said, searching for a more direct compliment, "I'm not bad myself."

A chime sounded as a green light came on in the pedestal between them. "Uh-Oh." Kelly frowned. "A call from the company means something's about to change. I'll get it."

"Ok" Bill said. "I'll taxi and talk to ground control. You find out what's up." Kelly nodded and applied herself to the other frequency taking notes as she went. The 757 made its turn into the gate area as the last baggage carts and catering trucks scurried out of its way. A mechanic stood on a tug in front of them and waved them into the gate in a symphony of lighted wands.

Bill slowed and began inching his way into the gate, sticking to the painted yellow line and lights to make certain the wings he couldn't see remained clear of obstacles. "Cut number one." He announced.

Kelly had completed her conversation and reached over to pull the fuel control switch on the left engine down. "Chop number one." she confirmed, completing the shutdown checklist. The big engine wound down and the jet slowed to a stop. Mechanics threw chocks under the massive wheels. A fuel truck jousted with baggage loaders and septic tank vehicles to position itself at the aircraft. The gate agent maneuvered the jetway up to the forward entry door as Shaheera, smiling elegantly, disarmed and opened it.

Back in the closed cockpit Kelly announced "Change in plans Bill. Hurry up and grab your stuff. The company wants us to rush over to the next concourse and take a turn-around to Cincinnati pronto. Her heart sank as she realized this meant she wouldn't be flying Fletcher to Washington.

Bill groaned. "What? No time to grab a quick bite to eat here? I'm starving!"

"No rest for the wicked Bill." Kelly commiserated "They have a full load of passengers over there who have been sitting for an hour. The pilots didn't show up. Their inbound flight had a mechanical problem."

Bill grumbled something unintelligible. They finished the shutdown checklists and began packing up their flight cases. Kelly unplugged her headset and hurriedly stuffed it into her flight kit.

By the time she finished and scrambled over the console to open the flight deck door everyone in the first class section was gone. Kelly was disappointed to find that this included Fletcher and his partner. She stared disconsolately at the empty seat as the rest of the coach passengers filed happily out in front of her.

"Get the lead out Kelly." Bill advised, pushing his way past her. "I'll go get the pre-flight started and meet you there if you'll finish saying our goodbyes here."

Kelly nodded to the back of his departing head and forced a smile as she thanked her deplaning passengers for flying with them. She knew that wherever Fletcher was he would be returning to this aircraft for the rest of the flight to Washington DC. Kelly didn't want to leave him wondering where she went again but couldn't bring herself to leave anything as forward as her phone number either. She didn't know what she wanted or expected. All she knew was that she had experienced something rare and personal with this exceptional man and he needed to know that.

Deciding that the rest of the passengers probably wouldn't miss her goodbyes she turned to Shaheera. "Shaheera I've got to run." Kelly said. "Change in scheduling for me. We have to take a turn around for another flight. Would you do me a big favor?"

"Anything for you. You know that."

"Thanks." Kelly smiled and began unfastening her gold pilot wings from her uniform jacket. Shaheera looked puzzled as Kelly took them off and placed them in her hand, folding her fingers tightly over them.

"I want you to make sure that the Federal Air Marshall who was sitting in seat 2A, Agent Eugene Fletcher, gets these. Tell him I wanted him to have my wings because of his dedication to serving and protecting our flight crews. Thank him for having my '6.

Shaheera's expression went from one of puzzlement to amusement and mischievousness. "Ooh, you mean that beautiful hunk of man sitting over there with those eyes?" she grinned. "Oh my yes. I'll be sure to do that and I'll tell him that the First Officer wants his body. Kelly girl, you do have good taste. I was beginning to worry that you'd joined a nunnery."

Kelly was mortified and the look she shot her friend quelled Shaheera's enthusiasm, dampening the megawatt smile. "I'm sorry Shaheera." Kelly apologized. I just want him to know that I appreciate something he did for me. I don't really know what else I want. I don't even know if he's married or not." Kelly gave Shaheera a quick hug and said "I'll treat you to dinner on our next layover and give you all of the juicy details then. How about that? Just make sure he gets the wings, and be professional."

Shaheera brightened considerably at the prospect of being privy to the love life of her very private friend. She hugged Kelly back and put the wings in her pocket. "You go on now. You know you can count on me." Shaheera stood at her most dignified parody of attention and whipped out a salute. Kelly hesitated. Shaheera made a "shooing" motion. "Go on!"

Kelly turned and picked up her bags. Trotting down the jetway at an awkward jog she called over her shoulder, "Thanks."

As Kelly disappeared around the corner Shaheera shouted "You're welcome and I want a lobster dinner!" Smiling to herself and patting Kelly's wings in her pocket Shaheera whispered "You just let your girlfriend decide what's best for you Kelly girl."

Kelly didn't know how many more times her heart could take running into Fletcher and then having to let him go again. She hurried toward the escalator dragging sixty pounds of flight case and travel bag behind her. Kelly slowed to a walk shaking her head at the irony. There by the Starbucks concession shop stood a familiar figure. He had his back to her and was talking casually to his partner while trying to blend in.

As if he could. Kelly thought. Fletcher's partner was leaning against the wall and looked up to see Kelly stop next to them. Fletcher turned as if he had eyes in the back of his head. He glanced down at her bags then back to her with a worried expression. Before he could say anything, Kelly reached out and touched his shoulder.

"Fletcher, I just wanted you to know that our cockpit crew has been rerouted. We won't be going to D.C. with you but there's something I'd like for you to have. I left it with our lead flight attendant Shaheera." Kelly hesitated not knowing what else to say in the scrutiny of Fletcher's partner.

"I'm sorry to hear that." Fletcher began awkwardly.

Kelly finished for him. "I've got to run. There's a full 767 loaded with angry people waiting for me. Thank you again and take care." She turned and disappeared down the escalator.

Damn. Fletch thought. *There she goes again.* He turned disgustedly back toward his departure gate. *That's what I get for thinking I could wait until we got to D.C to ask her out to dinner.*

Carl had been working with Fletcher long enough to know better than to ask questions when he was that deep in thought. By the time they reached the gate Fletch had made up his mind to use his FAM resources to track Kelly down. He knew it might be stretching the limits of appropriate Federal security information requests but he could justify it on a more than personal level. The fact that she was an airline pilot and had been tracked and assaulted by a group of heavily accented Middle Eastern men on a layover bothered him.

He remembered the face of the attacker he'd fought with. Fletch had also caught a brief glimpse of the armed knife wielding leader over his Sig gunsight. *That face was hard to forget. Particularly those eyes and the hatred etched around the thin mouth. I've seen that face somewhere before.* he thought. Fletch promised himself that he would go through the database of photos of suspected felons and terrorists as soon as he got back to headquarters. He had a bad feeling about this but nothing he could pin down.

The gate agent boarded Fletch and his partner long before beginning the usual boarding of passengers. No sooner did they enter the cabin than Shaheera pounced on him with pent-up glee. "Agent Fletcher." she drawled sweetly. "First Officer Hunter gave me orders to see that you received these." She took his hand and proudly laid Kelly's wings in it. "She said that it's to thank you for taking such good care of the flight crews. And something about having her '6."

Fletch stood staring at Kelly's wings, not knowing what to say.

"Isn't it highly unusual for a pilot to give someone their wings?" Carl blurted out.

"It is indeed." Shaheera answered. "It's a very high honor." Then she grinned evilly and leaned closer to Fletch. "Personally." she giggled. "I think she wants your body."

He stood stunned, still staring at the wings. Half embarrassed and half delighted at the possibility that it may have been a bit of both.

"Holy Moses." his blond partner blurted out "You're not wearing the fake wedding ring you always have on to keep the flight attendants away?" Carl and Shaheera cackled together like grade school cronies at their perceived discovery about their two friends. "They warned us about the flight attendants lusting after FAMs " Carl grinned, "but they didn't tell us in FAM school that the pilots would be after us too!" he snorted. Fletch jerked his head up and glared scathingly at his partner. The laughter died to a few embarrassed throat clearings as Fletch remembered why he usually wore the ring. *His ex-wife had left him for a wealthy lawyer four years ago while he'd been deployed overseas in Bosnia. She'd taken their two young children with her. The ring didn't apply anymore but wearing it had kept him out of trouble. He wondered why he'd slipped it off his finger and into his pocket when he saw Kelly in the museum.* That was a subject he didn't want to think about right now. Not with his clueless partner and Kelly's ribald but well-meaning friend hanging over him.

" If you see first officer Hunter again please tell her thank you and that I'm honored." Fletch said. Placing the gold wings gently in his pocket over his heart, he buttoned them securely in and sat down. He wanted to check on Kelly's security and to find out how to see her again.

Throughout the rest of the flight Fletcher would place his hand over his heart and feel her wings pressed reassuringly against it. He needed to do that to convince himself that all of this had really happened and to rekindle the warmth in his heart that hadn't been there in a long time.

Then Fletch would smile.

Chapter Eleven
Pilot Lounge

Feb. 21, 2001 / 7:52 pm MST / Salt Lake City, Utah

Delta Air Lines pilot lounge Salt Lake International Airport

"Pilots take no special joy in walking. Pilots like flying."

- **Neil Armstrong**

Kelly stood in the crew lounge, a familiar mixture of excitement and anticipation piquing her curiosity. She was tired and anxious to go home but this was an unexpected opportunity. The main attraction was a thick sheaf of new bids Son the pilot bulletin board. Kelly's close call with Bill's bad decision cinched the deal. If the seniority was right, she was going to upgrade to 757 /767 captain. It was time.

Watching her compatriots mill around in their black, white and gold uniforms made her think of a big flock of opinionated eagles. Someone hailed an old flying buddy with a hearty bellow and stampeded toward the group.

Answering good-natured bellows welcomed him. Maybe a "herd" of pilots would be more like it. Kelly thought affectionately. Her hand went to the spot where her wings had been. She smiled knowing that the wings that had been hers for so many years now had a home with Fletch. A bittersweet ache filled her chest.

"Hey Kelly!" a lantern-jawed co-pilot hollered. "When are you going to take a captain's bid on the seven-six and rescue me from these other left-seat tyrants?" She recognized him as her favorite first officer. They'd flown together when she was a Captain on the smaller Boeing 727s and 737s.

"Hey Animal." Kelly responded. "I've got requests from captains that want me to come rescue them from YOU." Feeling like a salmon swimming upstream, she elbowed her way to the front of the mob and joined him. The comforting press of her fellow pilots calmed the wired feeling running across her nerves. She managed to get close enough to see the available captain's positions.

Kelly's welcome hadn't always been a warm one with this pilot group. she recalled. *As their airline's first female pilot a decade or so ago, the personnel director had warned her that the all-male pilot group were refusing to fly with "a Gott-damned woman pilot."* Kelly had smiled and told the personnel director that she understood their fear and knee-jerk reactions.

"The pilot group doesn't know anything about me personally or my piloting skills and history." she'd replied. *I don't take it personally because it's not personal. It's the concept they're objecting to. Not me. Pilots don't like unknown factors in the cockpit. I'm an unknown factor. They're just frightened by the idea and confused about their own status as men if I'm also doing a job that's so deeply rooted in their own masculinity."* Kelly had added that it was her responsibility, not theirs, to be patient with them and set the mood in the cockpit. She knew they had to feel that they could trust her

for them to operate well and comfortably together as a flight crew.

Kelly's sense of humor and compassion had ultimately been her most powerful tool. It was just who she was. *Kelly's first experience in the pilot lounge resulted in her being surrounded by a circle of pilots. One of them had waved her over and begun introducing her to the other men as their first female pilot. The pilot introducing her had noticed a hostile Neanderthal-looking captain glaring at her from across the room. His unibrow almost covering his eyes in a scowl. Arms crossed over his chest.*

To Kelly's horror her host had grinned evilly and forcibly dragged the angry captain over to introduce him to her. "Harlin." he'd said. "This is our first female airline pilot. Kelly Hunter. Unibrow had looked her up and down, refusing her outstretched hand and said "I just want you to know I don't like female pilots!" Kelly had looked back with a serious face and replied "Harlan. I just want you to know there are some female pilots I can't stand either."

Harlin had stood there with a "the lights are on but nobody's home" look. Then he'd reluctantly taken her hand saying "In your case maybe I'll make an exception." Kelly had replied. "I appreciate that Harlin. I'll try not to let you down."

Everything had gradually changed for the better over the years as she continued to prove herself worthy of their trust by just being herself. Now the respect and support they showed her had swung to the other extreme. *It was almost embarrassing.* she thought. Knowing all too well her own faults and weaknesses. Most of what they said about her was true but some of the stories Kelly heard about herself had catapulted her into legendary status. She decided she could live with that.

Animal smacked her good-naturedly on the shoulder. "Stop staring at the bids like a bird in front of a snake." he laughed. "You know you want it." Kelly poked him back as she turned the pages. Six captain slots were available on the B757/767 in Salt Lake City. "Ow!" Animal clutched his arm feigning injury. "You're always so mean to me and

I'm always looking out for you." Kelly ignored him and mentally calculated her seniority. "You've been a captain on everything else." Animal said rubbing his supposedly injured arm. "Why haven't you taken the left seat on the 75/76 yet?"

"Because I got tired of being a junior captain on reserve and never being home with my son." Kelly said distractedly. "I finally got smart. I've been waiting until I'm senior enough to choose what and when I fly." She ran her finger under the small print. "This way I might even get Christmas or my son's birthday at home for a change. He's not going to be there forever."

"Don't wait too long to fly with me again." Animal jibed. "I'm still on the market." He wagged his finger at her. "I'll only wait for you so long before I'm captured by some short fat little 90-year-old lady who owns a liquor store." Kelly turned and gave him her best cold raised eyebrow look. He staggered back clutching his arm again in mock fear. "Ow!" he yelled prematurely as she moved her hand. She laughed and turned back to her reading.

"Suck it up Animal." she chuckled. "You are such a marshmallow!" Kelly knew he was anything but a marshmallow. Animal was one of the smartest and most well-read pilots at the airline. He just liked to play dumb. Kelly stood up. "OK Animal. You talked me into it. I'm taking a captain bid on the 767."

"When does training start?" another co-pilot asked covetously, still staring at the bid sheet.

"In a month. The first class is on March fifteenth." Dramatic groans went up from hopeful pilots who were junior to her. She'd just bumped one of them out of a captain slot. Kelly almost felt guilty. Almost. "Your time will come." She reassured them. "Besides, you wouldn't want to be a captain and have to fly with Animal spitting tobacco in a bottle here any time soon would you?" The competition muttered in begrudging agreement.

"At least you don't spit in a bottle." one of them acknowledged. This drew laughs from the rest. It was a known fact that Animal chewed tobacco. His infamous receptacle for the nasty habit traveled with him. The tobacco bottle battle had earned him a trip to the Chief Pilot's office more than once.

Animal grinned unrepentantly. Then his focus shifted from Kelly's face to her jacket. "What happened to your wings?" he asked. "You'd better not let the Chief Pilot catch you without them or you'll be taking my place in the hot seat."

"Must have lost them somewhere." she hedged. "I'll have a new pair ordered before my next flight." The last thing Kelly needed was to have Animal prying into why she'd given her wings away. Strategically shifting the conversation back to bids Kelly smiled at the crowd and said "See you guys after training."

"Thanks for the vote of confidence." She smiled at Animal. "I'd better go pick up my 25 pounds of training material if I'm going to justify your faith in me."

Kelly sat down to program her request for the captain's opening into the nearest computer. She took a deep breath and began her mental pep talk. *I am going to have fun playing with the company's multi-million dollar simulators.* she lied to herself. The technology that made flying simulators as challenging as being in a real jet prevented lethal training mistakes. The motion, sound and visual simulator experience was so effective pilots often forgot it wasn't the real aircraft they were flying and suffered all of the same stress's and anxiety they would have endured during actual multiple emergencies in the air. It was designed that way on purpose. The course would be anything but a cake-walk. It wasn't meant to be easy. You could lose your job if you failed it. Kelly would be testing her skills against nightmare scenarios and multiple emergencies that were too dangerous to train for in real airplanes. Her job depended on overcoming them.

A roar of laughter exploded behind Kelly. Glancing over her shoulder, she watched the group amuse themselves with the continued antics of Animal. He'd snatched a gold-encrusted hat from the head of a graying captain and was attempting to place it on a flustered young marine. The new-hire flapped his hands at it in an effort to ward it off. Retrieving his cap, the captain ran his fingers through his leonine head of hair and settled it firmly back on his head. He gave Animal a warning look. More laughter ensued. Kelly turned back to her thoughts.

She closed her eyes, leaned back in her chair and continued her internal reprogramming. A positive attitude was essential to success in training. *This is going to be a great way to hone my skills and make me a better pilot.* she told herself. Still talking to herself Kelly went to the publication room and started picking out her study guides. Kelly crammed what books she could into her suitcase and headed for home. *No more flying into hurricanes. That fourth gold stripe won't look bad on the sleeve either*. she thought. It was one vanity she'd have to earn the right to.

Chapter Twelve
Call Me "Bob"

Feb. 22, 2001 / 09:15 am EST / Washington, DC

"Man does not live by words alone, despite the fact that he sometimes has to eat them."

- Adlai Stevenson

Two thousand miles to the East Fletch rolled out of his bed in Washington D.C. He had enjoyed his first PTSD free peaceful night's sleep in years. Today he was a man with a mission. The first thing that met his eyes was the gold set of wings on his dresser. He looked up in the mirror behind them and saw the face of an unshaven but happy man. The lines that had been etched by years of sorrow and quiet desperation had softened. There was a new fire in his eyes. He grinned and stretched contentedly. Then he got up and padded across the rough carpet of his government-issued quarters to the bathroom. Fletch was one of the small cadre' of thirty-two Federal Air Marshals who secretly patrolled the commercial airlines. The government didn't feel that the threat of hijacking in the US was valid enough to justify the expense of more FAMs.

He turned on the hot water in the shower and planned his day. *The first stop,* he thought, *will be the office of my buddy "Bob."* Fletch was at the top of the FAM food chain, being assigned to the Washington Field Office. His friend "Bob" was the FAM Representative for the National Security Council at the White House Situation Room. That office authorized Lt. Colonel Robert S. Blakely II to run any kind of check on anybody. Fletch flipped a hand into the steaming spray and stepped inside. Grabbing a handful of Yucca shampoo he lathered it through his long dark hair. Lt. Col. Robert Blakely II would never tolerate anyone else calling him Bob. Only Fletcher.

Fletch rinsed the lather out and chuckled as he remembered the incident. *They had been working their way back to base during a covert river crossing in Chechnya. Colonel Robert S. Blakely II had found the only loose boulder in the riverbank, slipped and knocked himself out, almost drowning. Fletcher had found Robert bobbing face down in the river and hoisted the unconscious Lt. Colonel up onto his back and carried him to the safety of the tree line.* "Bob" was their private joke. Fletch had never presumed to collect on the debt of a life saved. *Today.* he thought. *I have a favor to ask that will be right up old Bob's alley.*

Stepping out of the shower Fletch scrubbed his skin briskly with a dry towel and wrapped it around his waist. He grabbed his cell phone and moved to the couch where he sat down and punched in a coded number. Stretching his arm comfortably over the backrest, he swung his legs up on the cushions. A gruff voice on the other end answered.

"Blakely." it growled. "Speak."

"Bob?" Fletch grinned into the phone. He was enjoying this too much for his own good. The phone erupted in expletives then subsided into a genuinely happy series of colorful greetings. Fletch momentarily removed the phone from his ear, shaking back a wet strand of hair.

"Fletch you old Night Hunter." the voice blasted away. "Where the Hell have you been? How the Hell have you been?" The voice hesitated and became softer. "I haven't heard from you since, well, since that social climbing-money-grubbing so-called wife of yours, well, er, what can this old war dog do for you?"

Recovering from the unexpected painful memories of his ex-wife, Fletch apologized to his old friend. "I'm sorry Bob. I didn't realize it had been so long. I guess I just didn't know what to say." He swung his legs down from the couch. Running his fingers through his wet hair, he fought the tightness between his shoulder blades.

"There's nothing to say old buddy." the voice replied. "You loved her. You saved her from a violent ex-husband. She used you to escape for money and security."

"I know." Fletch whispered.

Bob hesitated as if unsure of the appropriateness of continuing. Fletch's brief silence proved an irresistible temptation to the Lt. Colonel. He continued mercilessly. "I told you what I thought when you were so intent on marrying her but you always did believe the best of people. You're just a damn hero intent on rescuing everybody." There was some nervous throat clearing on the other end of the line, then a distracted "Always were."

Fletch sat in chastised discomfort before hearty laughter filled the silence. "Well Hell you romantic redskin." Bob allowed. "If you weren't always playing the hero I guess they'd be calling me 'Bubbles' instead of 'Bob'."

Fletch heard the anger subsiding in his friend's voice. You're better off without her." the Lt. Colonel continued. "I'm just sorry she's got that lawyer husband of hers making it so hard for you to see your kids."

"Thanks." Fletch said. "That's quite an intelligence network you've got working for you Bob. I didn't know I was such a celebrity on the Washington grapevine."

"Don't worry. You're not." Bob said smugly. "It's my job to know things and the grapevine says that you've been too much of a hermit for my liking. Is there any special lady in your life to patch up that wound in your heart?"

Fletch felt his muscles relax and a weight lift from his shoulders. The mood lightened with thoughts of Kelly. "I was actually calling to ask a favor and collect on a small debt." he responded. "If my hunch is right, we might even put some of the bad guys out of business before they can do any damage."

"So, who's doing whom the favor again?" Bob asked. "I can't stand owing you another one. It's too humiliating. What's this all about anyway?" Fletch could hear him settling his ear intently into the phone as he anticipated the hunt.

"The last mission I ran to Seattle." Fletch answered. "I got into it with what appeared to be three potential Tangos who tracked and attempted to assault a Delta pilot on a layover. I think they were after ID. We managed to fight them off but they got away. Fletch hesitated, waiting for Bob to respond. "Why do you think terrorists would be interested in an airline pilot's ID badge?" Bob asked. Fletch said "I'm not sure why, but the airlines sent a security bulletin out two months ago cautioning all their flight crews to be careful on layovers because someone has been stealing their ID badges and uniforms from their rooms. I don't like it Bob. They never do anything without a reason. Something big involving the airlines may be coming. I'd like to have access to the CIA's International terrorist database system." Fletch hesitated. "I think that I can identify at least two of them."

There was a long silence on the other end of the phone then a low whistle.

"If what you say turns out to be the case we've got a problem." Bob stated. "That's a damned stupid move for a Tango cell to make though, don't you think? Why would they take a chance like that and draw attention to themselves just to get a pilot's ID?"

Fletch could hear him tapping a tooth with his fingernail. A habit Bob had when deep in concentration.

"What makes you think they were anything other than ordinary hoodlums out for some quick cash?" Bob continued. "Now that I think about it, why were you and this airline pilot chumming around on a layover anyway? You know you're supposed to keep a low profile." he said reprovingly.

"Actually," Fletch countered, "we bumped into each other at the Seattle Asian Museum of Art and found a common interest in Japanese bows and Katanas. Neither one of us was aware of what the other did for a living until considerably later. That's when the red flags went up for me on this situation."

"Ah. That explains one part of the question," Bob allowed, "but why do you think they may be Tangos?

"The attack was well planned and executed. They apparently followed the pilot to a coffee shop and waited there for an hour. Then followed the pilot for another half hour by car. They waited for three hours outside of the museum for the pilot to come out. They all appeared to be of Middle Eastern descent. Not locals. They were well dressed and they spoke Farsi and Dari, Bob. We know that's an obscure language used in terrorist training camps in Afghanistan." Fletch let that sink in. "We've had security alerts out regarding that Bin Laden Saudi for the last year. He's shown an inordinate interest in airlines."

When the FAM Liaison spoke again his voice was lower and quieter. "It doesn't look good does it? You come in to see me today at my office."

Fletch leaned forward in anticipation. "Where?"

"You do remember where I am in the old Eisenhower Building on Pennsylvania Avenue don't you? I'll have all the access you need to the CIA's TTIC database…Photos, fingerprints, dossiers. You name it and it's yours."

"Thanks Bob." Fletch said. "I appreciate it. How about grabbing some breakfast first?"

"Make it lunch and you're on." his friend offered. "That will give me time to pull the necessary strings for you."

Bob's in his element now. Fletch thought. *I can hear it in his voice*. "Sounds good. I'll see you at noon at that Mexican Restaurant in Georgetown. The one the Spooks like to frequent." Fletch was about to hang up when Bob stopped him.

"By the way, that pilot, how did he handle himself in the fight?" he asked. "Those jet jockeys usually haven't done any hand-to-hand combat practice since their early military training. Did you have to do all the fighting and rescue the wussie's butt?" he laughed.

"Actually," Fletch replied. "She's almost six feet tall, long blond hair, beautiful and a nineteen-year veteran of the martial arts. She appreciated my help but was rescuing her own very fine butt just dandy."

Fletch was thoroughly enjoying the astounded silence on the other end of the line. He liked it even more when Bob started sputtering and demanding to know exactly what the relationship was and where it was heading.

"You'll just have to hurry up and get me that database access Bob. I'll give you the details over lunch. Bye." Fletch grinned and punched the off button on his cell phone.

Chapter Thirteen
The Cell

Feb. 22, 2001 / 07:30 am EST / Tampa, Florida

"I was struck by the joy of those pilots in committing cold-blooded murder... Frankly, this is not cojones. This is cowardice."

- Madeline Albright, U.S. Ambassador to the U.N.,1996

Atta and a hungover Rasheed filed out of the United Airlines Regional jet and into the air-conditioned terminal in Venice Florida. They'd taken the red-eye flight from Seattle to Miami. Then they waited two hours before catching a short commuter flight to their final destination. The view from the terminal was cheery and tropical. A brilliant blue sky and flowering plants threw hues of red, gold and green everywhere. Glimpses of translucent turquoise ocean were just visible under puffy white clouds to the West. Atta and Rasheed pushed through the mob of colorfully clad vacationers.

"Come." Atta prodded his lagging companion and strode off. Rasheed glanced at the happy faces and wondered what it would be like to have so much freedom and so few cares. He obeyed and stepped up his pace.

Rasheed's life as a physical education teacher in Saudi Arabia had not helped his chronic depression. Only when his doctor had prescribed memorizing the Quran and praying to Mecca five times a day did he feel that his life had a purpose. He looked at Atta striding on ahead of him. The envy turned to resentment as he consoled himself that these lucky people were all infidels and deserving of the divine wrath that he served. *Surely, he, Rasheed, would have all of this and more in paradise for his devotion to Allah and the Jihad.*

The three vodka tonics he'd accepted on the flight had made his worries vanish and given him a few hours of sleep. Now they were turning into a pounding headache. He prayed to Allah to have mercy and take this punishment away. He was only following orders for the sake of the Jihad when he consumed alcohol.

Atta motioned to Rasheed and headed toward the rental car kiosks. Rasheed followed miserably in his wake. The terrorist leader kept his eyes straight ahead and avoided looking at the scantily clad females corrupting the space around him. Even as a young boy Atta would leave the room when his conservative Muslim family selected a television station tuned to belly dancing. *Women are unclean things.* he thought. *We will stop and purify ourselves with prayer as soon as we get to Highway 41.* This place sickened him, but he would stay and complete his holy mission. Stoking the anger inside he reminded himself. *I am the wrath of Allah incarnate.* Setting his mouth in a grim line he drew on his mathematical engineer's mind and self-discipline.

I am the shining knight of a new Caliphate. he recited. *Loyal Jihadis will ensure that pure Islam will once again rule the world. It will burn this Western cancer of America, Israel and their allies from the earth.* He felt better after reassuring himself of his purpose.

Atta stopped at the rental car desk and smiled at the young woman behind it. "I have a reservation for a rental car." he stated and gave her his assumed name. Rasheed mimicked a weak smile beside him.

"Certainly sir." she beamed citing the company slogan. "It's our job to make your job easier." Shuffling efficiently through the contracts she found his and handed him the keys.

Driving south towards the small town of Venice lifted Atta's spirits as he watched the ocean play hide and seek between the tropical trees and tourist towns. Constant prayer and study for flight training would be a welcome and familiar regimen for him.

I will continue my classes at Huffman Aviation tomorrow. he decided. *It will be good to see Marwan again.*

Atta's self-absorbed silence and the air-conditioned comfort of the Ford soothed Rasheed's aching head. He began to relax.

When Atta pulled over at a truck stop for orange juice and prayer Rasheed's hangover had abated.

Later that afternoon they drove into the parking lot of Huffman Aviation at Venice Airport. Another rented Escort parked beside them. Atta told Rasheed to stay in the car while he got out and spoke with the occupant of the other vehicle.

Rasheed had never felt comfortable with these unexpected newcomers. Seeing what had happened to Wail made him even more nervous. He relaxed when he recognized the other man as an acquaintance from the Afghanistan training camps. Marwan Al-Shehhi was in the driver's seat of the other car. Al Shehhi had always been friendly toward him. Rasheed wondered how Marwan had managed to endure living with the stoic Atta for so long. He supposed that the company of the other men who shared their quarters and went to the same Mosques made it bearable. They had all attended the University of Hamburg. *These "Hamburg Men" have met with Osama bin Laden.* he reminded himself. *They are part of an elite group selected for a special assignment against America.* Rasheed had come hoping to be included.

Atta opened the driver's door and slid back inside in a cloud of hot humid air. "There has been a change of plans." Atta announced. "Our fourth pilot has been found and is taking further training in San Diego."

Rasheed crumbled inwardly. *Where did this leave him?* Looking at the flat black eyes of his leader he thought he could see a flicker of humor in the brittle mask of his features.

"Have no fear brother." Atta added benignly "You will go back to Afghanistan with honor for further training as muscle in this mission. I will see you again in the Spring. You will not be denied your place in history or in Paradise."

Rasheed had never seen Atta behave in such a benevolent manner. "Thank you, Mohammed." he said. Somehow, he actually believed him. *Something truly good must have happened to bring on this flood of generosity.* Rasheed thought. "Then all is well and I am no longer needed for training as a pilot here?" Rasheed asked.

"Allah is merciful and his will is inevitable." Atta proclaimed. We are sending another Jihadi, Zacarias Moussaoui, to study as a backup pilot in Norman Oklahoma." Atta made a sour face. Rasheed thought it was disturbingly similar to his normal expression lately. "Ziad Jarrah is already completing his studies at the flight school next door." he continued. It was no secret that Atta disapproved of Jarrah's Westernized Muslim wife Aysel and thought her a security risk. Everyone also knew that the back-up pilot, Moussaoui, was a hothead and not the sharpest tool in the shed. His only redeeming quality was that he desperately wanted to kill Americans and that his French passport allowed him easy access to the U.S. to do so.

As if reading Wail's thoughts Atta added "The fourth pilot, Hani Hanjour, has been in America for years. He has a US pilot rating and was recently recruited."

"Why does he join us?" Rasheed asked.

"He is disappointed that neither the American or the Saudi Airlines will hire him and has given himself to our holy cause." Atta made what passed for a smile. "Allah provides and all is indeed well."

By noon the next day Mohammed el-Amir Atta and Marwan al-Shehhi were both hitting the books again at Huffman Aviation. The courses would take them through their private and commercial pilot's licenses. They were renting a room from the bookkeeper at the flight school and had long ago set up their bank accounts and cell phones. Several wire transfers of $70,000.00 had already been received. Other than the fact that they had all lied about losing their passports to erase any record of the countries they had traveled to, everything was perfectly legal.

Atta had nothing but contempt for how easily manipulated a nation like America was with its personal rights. *Such stupid things will not be tolerated in Islam.* he reassured himself. *They will be the death of America.*

Rasheed had been shepherded to another Al Qaeda safe house in Hollywood Florida to be flown back to Afghanistan. He was booked through the normal series of diversionary flights. London, Prague, Saudi Arabia and Pakistan.

That night Atta and al-Shehhi tossed the last of their cheap pizza crusts on the floor. Atta turned from his aviation books and announced it was time for evening prayers. His mind may have been orderly but his personal habits had become appalling during the last few weeks. They knelt among scraps of old food, candy wrappers and discarded clothing to commune with Allah.

Al-Shehhi lay down on the small bed by the noisy swamp cooler as midnight approached. His snoring soon joined the air conditioner in a discordant duet. Atta got up and turned the machine off. Then he sat down in the hard-backed chair under the glare of the lamp by the window. His body settled rigidly in position and he focused his attention on the aviation text. He glanced at Kelly's bid package. It was becoming a touchstone to him. He had a purpose and he was in control.

The numbers and formulas required to pilot an aircraft put him in his element as a student of engineering. There was no confusing human empathy or human weakness here. Numbers were the language of God. Atta felt invincible.

Chapter Fourteen
"Spook" Central

Feb. 22, 2001 / 12:00 pm EST / Washington, DC La Puerta restaurant

"Listen, Pilgrim! There are no roads. Roads are made by walking."

- Richard Rohr

Fletcher's mouth watered at the scent of freshly baked tortillas. He walked into La Puerta and let his eyes adjust to the dimly lit interior. *Spook Central.* He thought. *If you want to know who's CIA or FBI, look for the rumpled accountant type or movie star elegance. They seemed to go for extremes.* A casual survey of the occupants confirmed his opinion. Brightly decorated tables were populated with drab accountants and a few glamorous individuals who seemed to have wandered in from Monaco by mistake. Fletch felt that the accountant types were by far the most formidable.

Two individuals didn't fit the mold. They were sitting at a corner table. The larger of the pair sported a silver-grey crew cut. When he saw Fletch, he raised his hand and beckoned him over. The sleeves of Bob's white business shirt were rolled up over his thick muscular forearms.

"One for lunch sir?" A pretty Latino girl smiled hopefully at Fletch.

"No." he answered. "I'm joining the two gentlemen in the corner." he gestured with his chin. "Thanks anyway. Fletch headed for the table. "Bob?" he grinned. "Your hair's a bit shorter than the last time I saw you but you still look like a pit bull on steroids. Peggy must be taking good care of you."

Bob stood up and gripped Fletcher's hand. "Yes she is you old Night Hunter and you look thinner. You're in serious need of one of her home-cooked meals." Noticing Fletcher's inquiring look he turned and introduced the clean-cut man sitting at his table. "Eugene Fletcher, I'd like you to meet another friend of mine. Lt. Colonel Joe Johnson. He's with U.S. Army Intelligence and the National Security Agency."

Pushing aside a bowl of chips, the trim man stood and offered his hand. "It's a pleasure to finally meet you Fletcher. Robert speaks highly of you."

Fletch shook his hand. It was firm and dry.

"The pleasure is mine sir." Fletch responded. He stepped back and resumed his appraisal of the men. "Two Lieutenant Colonels and one lowly FAM Drill Sergeant?" he commented. "I'm beginning to feel a little out-ranked here."

"Sorry to spring this on you at the last minute." the Intelligence officer said. "Colonel Blakely called me this morning and suggested that we all meet for lunch so I took advantage of the opportunity to have him buy."

Fletch knew that there was more to it than that but he liked the man's style. "If I'd known that you were buying," Fletch joined in, "I would have suggested a more expensive restaurant."

"If I'd known I was buying." Bob frowned. "I would have ordered pizza in my office." The waitress appeared to take their orders. After she left, Bob broached the subject.

"Fletch I've known Joe since OCS. He can be trusted to remain off the record. I also think that he can shorten your database search considerably." Bob took a sip of ice water and scooped a huge pile of salsa onto his tortilla chip. He attacked the food with gusto.

The Intelligence officer leaned forward on his elbows resuming the conversation where Bob had left off. "Robert gave me the details of why you needed to search our terrorist database. You and I might have run across the same individuals. It's just a hunch but if I'm right you'd be helping me as well."

Fletch felt like he'd hit the jackpot but it was too soon to get excited. "That would be a real find." he said. "Any help that I can give you by identifying these guys I will. It might amount to nothing but I'm not willing to take that chance."

"I agree." Joe said. "Experience has taught me to trust my instincts."

Muffled choking from Bob interrupted the conversation. "Hey Bob. Salsa too spicy?" Joe asked. Your eyeballs appear to be sweating."

"That's Robert to you." Bob rasped, frantically motioning the waitress to refill his water glass. "Just-got-some down the wrong pipe." he wheezed.

"Probably better to enjoy the meal here and discuss business later anyway." Joe suggested, indicating the room with a faint tilt of his head.

The waitress scurried to their table and refilled Bob's glass. Then she slid the platters of food in front of them. "I think better on a full stomach." Fletch said. "This is breakfast for me. I'm starving. Let's eat." He had to consciously control his impatience to get to the database but he understood Joe's need for confidentiality. The food was a welcome distraction.

They left the waitress a generous tip and Joe handed the cashier his Visa. "Don't worry Robert." he grinned. "I'm getting the better part of the deal. I'll pay."

The ride up Pennsylvania Avenue to the brooding grey facade of the Old Eisenhower Building seemed interminable. Bob drove like he lived. Aggressively defying the laws of God and physics. They parked in a reserved slot and entered via a high-security door. After the guards checked his credentials Fletch followed the two officers up to Robert Blakely's small but tasteful office. The look was Washingtonian Brass all the way. A smartly dressed middle-aged secretary behind the dark oak desk brightened as they came in.

"Hold my calls for a bit Sheryl." Bob instructed. "I'll be in a meeting for an hour or so."

"Yes Sir. Will you want coffee, water or soft drinks?" she asked.

"Just water, I think. Thank you, Sheryl."

"Gentlemen." he gestured. Ushering them in and closing the door behind them. "Please make yourselves comfortable."

The NSA officer went directly to the computer and sat down at Bob's desk. He'd obviously been here before. The room was rife with anticipation as Joe took a strange-looking encryption unit from his briefcase and plugged it into the USB port on Bob's computer. His fingers hit several more keystrokes and the screen flashed with a Cover Sheet entitled "Defense Intelligence Agency" in bold face lettering. Below that rested the Seal of the U.S. Army and subtext announcing "U.S. Military Intelligence Alpha Danger CTS Database Files."

Joe swiveled around to face Fletch. "Don't look so worried." he smiled. "This is classified but not beyond your security clearance. The powers that be place relatively little importance on counter-terrorism within the United States." he said. He got up from the black leather chair and offered it to Fletch. "I'm not going to tell you anything about what I know until you've had a look at these files. Just pull up each page of photos by clicking on the arrow. Take your time." he said. "We'll compare notes later if you find anything."

"Thanks." Fletch acknowledged, sitting down and swiveling to face the screen. He scrolled to the first page of swarthy faces. It brought back memories of Kelly and the attack in the alley. The knowledge of what might happen to her if he was right hardened his resolve. "At least I'll be able to sleep nights one way or the other." he added.

"That will make two fewer insomniacs if you find what I'm thinking you will." Joe responded. He and Bob seated themselves on an overstuffed couch against the far wall. The leather creaked as they sat down and conversed in hushed tones.

Fletch began scrutinizing the first set of faces. By the second page he had identified three well-known terrorists. They weren't the men in the alley but they bore a passing resemblance. *I recognize these guys from FAM security training*, he thought. The bearded and clean-shaven versions of Khalid Sheikh Mohammed stared half-lidded at him.

A two-million-dollar reward for capture was listed in the small print below. Fletch was familiar with the fact that this man had attempted to blow up a dozen U.S. Civilian Airliners over the Pacific in 1995. It had been a matter of luck that a co-conspirator, Ramzi Yousef, had set fire to himself and the Manila apartment where he was making the bombs. Only Yousef's clumsiness had prevented the airliner plot from blossoming into a horrifying reality.

Fletch stifled a bitter laugh as he remembered that Ramzi Yousef had also gotten himself hospitalized in a car crash during his aborted attempt to blow up a car bomb in the basement of the World Trade Center in 1992. The subsequent successful bombing was so slipshod that the CIA had dubbed him an "ad Hoc Terrorist."

It was pure luck that police investigating the fire found a computer detailing the airliner plot. *These guys were getting better with experience*. Fletch bit back the frustration of knowing that most of the terrorists involved had easily bumbled or slithered their way out of arrest. They were still busy "making Chocolate" (as Yousef called his bomb construction) elsewhere.

He scrolled through more photographs of Middle Eastern men. Some had sad faces. Some had happy faces. Some of them looked like a friend you would meet on your way to the store. Fletch controlled his natural curiosity about their dossiers and stayed focused on the task at hand. His gaze passed over the Terrorist Poster-Boy's visage of a bearded Osama bin Laden. A quote from his Comanche Grandfather raced through his thoughts. *"The devil says 'My best work is done in the name of the Great Spirit'."* He shook his head at the truth in that.

Bringing up the next page Fletch felt a prickly sensation. The dead black eyes and rigid features staring out at him had an unpleasant familiarity. He hit the enlarge key and leaned closer. It had been foggy and dimly lit but he could almost hear the cold flat voice issuing demands in the alley.

Yes! Those eyes and that slash of a mouth. There had been just enough light as Fletch aimed his Sig Saur. The man had turned slightly towards him. "Colonel Johnson?" Fletch said, eyes still frozen on the screen.

Joe was peering over Fletcher's shoulder in an instant. Fletch looked up in time to catch a glimmer of what looked like triumph in his eyes. Bob towered over them both.

"Look familiar to you?" Joe asked.

"Not an easy face to forget." Fletch answered. "I got a quick look at this one over the sight of my gun. He seemed to be running the show."

Joe nodded. "Interesting." he stated. "Why don't you run through the rest of the file and see if you recognize any more of your dancing partners? Then we can compare notes."

Elated, Fletch bent to the task, saved the photo and continued scrolling. He took a sip of water from the cut crystal glass and clicked onto the next page. "There!" he said, setting the glass down and pointing at a scowling young man. "The last time I saw this one he was bleeding and his nose was swollen." Fletch grinned wolfishly and rubbed his knuckles at the memory.

"I guess we can call that one a definite ID can't we?" Joe laughed.

"I'll wager he remembers you vividly as well." Bob added.

"You said that there was also a third man involved? The one that initiated the attack on the pilot." Joe continued. "Want to finish the database photos and see if he turns up as well?"

Fletch shook his head and turned to meet Joe's eyes. "Sorry but it wouldn't do any good. I came onto the scene rather abruptly, about the time he left. Only the pilot got a look at him."

"Did you get a description?" Joe asked hopefully.

"No, but I had every intention of discussing the details with her at a later date in a calmer setting." Fletch rubbed the back of his neck. His eyes seemed to focus on a memory. "She had a habit of running away every time the opportunity presented itself."

Chapter Fifteen
The Night Hunter

*Feb. 22, 2001 / 2:20 pm EST / Washington,
DC Office of Lt. Colonel Robert (Bob)
Blakely, FAM coordinator NSC*

**"He who wants to protect everything,
protects nothing" is one of the
fundamental rules of defense.**

- **Lt. General Adolf Galland,
Luftwaffe.**

"God knows I tried, but she was always moving too fast for me to get her phone number." Fletch said. Regret laced his voice.

Putting his hands in his pockets, Joe studied his shoes for a moment. "Maybe we can remedy that. Meanwhile, I'm going to tell you, off the record, why I was looking for these gentlemen." He sat in one of the wingback chairs next to Bob. Then he rested his elbows on his knees and began.

"I represent a secret intelligence gathering unit of the U.S. Military. Our mission is to identify potential terrorist threats to this country using data mining techniques. We operate on a Black Budget. He paused as if deciding whether to continue or not. Decision already made, he forged ahead. "The first man that you identified as the leader is an Egyptian student of Engineering. He's spent quite a bit of time among a radical sect of Islam in the Al Quds Mosque in Hamburg, Germany. He's also attended Terrorist Training camps in Afghanistan sponsored by Osama bin Laden."

"What was he doing stalking an Airline Pilot in Seattle?" Fletch asked. "Who is this guy?"

Joe motioned for patience.

"That's where you come in. His real name is Mohamed Mohamed el-Amir Awad el-Sayed Atta. We've been tracking him and several other members of a potential terrorist cell inside the U.S. for the past six months. His passport has been reissued numerous times. The latest in the name of Mohamed Atta. Two months ago he and other members of this cell just disappeared. They dropped off the radar screen altogether."

He leaned forward and looked at Fletch. "You my friend, have just found Atta and at least one of the other members of his cell for me. They're evidently up to no good in Seattle if they're going to this much trouble stalking airline flight crews."

Fletch felt both vindicated and worried. His eyes widened at the realization of what this meant. "What about my punching bag?" he asked. "Is he another big player in this?"

"Not really." Joe responded. "He's just a recent addition to the group. He's more of a disgruntled follower than a leader. With this group you never know. I'm not getting anywhere working within the system."

"What do you mean?" Fletch asked, feeling a cold chill creep up his spine. Bob was uncharacteristically quiet.

"I mean," said Joe, "that I've pulled out the stops to try to get this to the FBI or CIA and enlist their help here. Our own military lawyers won't let us share the information with any other agency so we're basically FUBAR'd."

Bob snorted in derision, "What the Hell kind of legal reasoning prompted that?"

"Much as I hate to play the devil's advocate," Joe sighed. "Technically they've broken no laws. Since they're here legally on student visas they're entitled to the same rights of privacy and liberty under the law as a US citizen. Our legal department feels that any surveillance or arrests would blow up in our faces."

Fletch and Bob looked at each other in disbelief.

"I know." Joe said catching their looks. "Another officer from Naval Intelligence and I made several unsuccessful attempts to change their minds." He looked at Bob. "You know how bad the FBI and CIA are about sharing anything. Everyone's so busy guarding their own territory we're missing leads all over the place."

"So where do we go from here without disobeying orders or creating a security breach?" Fletch asked. "Just how dangerous do you think these guys really are?"

"Let me put it this way." Joe said, looking from one man to another. "We know that Atta and his Hamburg group met with Osama bin Laden near the start of Ramadan last Fall in Kandahar. Two of Bin Laden's close advisors also attended. Maybe you know them. Khalid Sheikh Mohamed and his friend Ramzi Yousef."

"I'm familiar." Fletch said grimly. Bob nodded.

"We haven't had much luck getting a mole into Bin Laden's network but we believe that the subject of their discussion was commercial aircraft within the United States." Joe wagged his pen pointedly at Fletch. "What you've just told me pretty much confirms what they're up to. They're considering some sort of terrorist hijacking or bombing activity involving the airlines and the U.S. You FAMs are usually on International Flights only. Am I right?"

Fletch nodded.

"Can we arrest them on the basis of testimony from Fletch and the pilot regarding the assault?" Bob suggested hopefully.

"That would be convenient, wouldn't it?" Joe said. "Up until now we didn't even know where they were. Their last known whereabouts were another radical mosque in New Jersey. Then they dropped out of sight again. They appear to travel extensively." He looked at Bob. "At least now we can try to pick up the trail in Seattle. Frankly, I don't think the accusation will stand with our legal department. Our first order of business will be to find them again."

"What are the odds they're still in Seattle?" Bob asked.

"Pretty poor considering their run-in with your Federal Air Marshal and the pilot." Joe answered. "They're getting less careless all of the time. Unless they're exceedingly stupid they will have realized their mistake and gotten out of town." Bob was tapping his tooth again. Joe addressed Fletch, who was looking more concerned by the minute. "Didn't you say that the pilot was a female?"

"Yes." Fletch responded. "Why do you ask?"

"Because Atta's usually a very logical thinker." Joe stated. "His personality profile indicates that he's a calculating sort. Highly intelligent. Narcissist, OCD and a control freak. Bordering on sociopath. He has no social life. Everything centers on his religion and hatred of Israel, America, and anyone who doesn't share his radical beliefs." Joe let that sink in. "Where your pilot is concerned, I think she triggered something that caused him to make an emotion-based mistake."

Before Fletch or Bob could ask the obvious question, he answered it. "With the exception of his mother, Atta detests women. Your female airline pilot represents a woman in a position of power. Atta would view this as a direct challenge to himself and Islam. He'd be driven to take her down." Joe said grimly. "You could say that she's his Achilles heel. He'd also view her as an easy victim. In his mind this would only be...logical." Joe stood and rested both hands on the desk. "We can use this against him."

Fletch felt sick.

"What I'm going to ask you to do is also off the record and not sanctioned by my office or by the US government." Joe continued. "You know the drill. This meeting never happened. I'll deny ever discussing this with you." Turning to Fletch, Joe looked apologetic but determined.

"I'd like for you to arrange a meeting with your pilot and have her scan the photos that you just looked at, minus the data. If she can identify the third attacker, who knows? It may just be the key to finding the whereabouts of Atta's cell before something bad happens."

Fletch looked at Bob who nodded in assent. There was a sadness in his eyes that alarmed Fletch. He looked back at the intelligence officer. "Can I tell her what this is about?" he asked. Already knowing the answer.

"I'm sorry Fletcher but no, you cannot." Joe stated. "This is classified material. That alone would merit a no. We're doing this off the record and walking a very thin line between insubordination and doing our jobs. You can better protect the pilot by getting the information we've asked you for from her." Joe attempted an encouraging smile. "Let us follow up on it to get to Atta. Can you do that?"

Fletch felt anger boiling up as he realized the implications of what the Intelligence officer had said. His muscles tensed. "What you're telling me is that you want me to get information from her and then let her go about her business as usual, unaware that she's a target? You want to use her as bait for Atta." Fletcher's fingers curled into fists. Bob laid a bear-sized paw on his arm. Fletch whipped his head around to glare at his friend and saw the concern in his eyes. It deflated his urge to deck Joe. He took a deep breath and sank back in his chair.

"Sorry." Fletch apologized. Wondering what had come over him. "I see your point and yes I can do that." He still felt a knot in his stomach and his lunch was no longer sitting well with him.

Surprise swelled across the Intelligence officer's face as he glanced from Fletch to Bob and back. He straightened his tie and a look of understanding crossed his features. "Am I right in assuming that this lady airline pilot may be more than just Attas's weak link?" he asked.

The answer was written on Fletcher's face.

"You know that we can't help her if we let ourselves get emotionally involved in this don't you?" Joe eyed Fletch with suspicion. "I can't let you work with me if you think you might alert her to anything. You're also aware of that?"

"Yes sir." Fletch acknowledged in a voice quieter than Bob had ever heard him. "Of course you're right. I'll do whatever it takes to help you get these guys before they can harm this country." he forced a smile.

"Good. I'll have the Delta company mail address where you can contact this Kelly

Hunter later today." Joe was silent for a moment. "I do understand how difficult it is to remain detached when someone you care about is involved." he said.

Fletch sat in stunned defeat. Staring at nothing. *I care about her.* he realized. He'd been trying not to care about anyone for a long time. "Thank you." he said. "I'll get back to you as soon as I have anything to report."

"I'll be waiting." Joe responded. "You're doing the right thing." he reassured Fletch.

Bob started to put his hand on Fletcher's shoulder, thought better of it and awkwardly patted his back. "You're doing the right thing Fletcher." he confirmed.

"I'll drive you back to your place."

"Gentlemen, I'll be in touch." Joe said. He picked up his briefcase and headed for the door.

Feeling numb, Fletch allowed himself to be shepherded back to the car. Bob looked like he was trying to figure out if he should open the door for Fletch or not.

"Try it and I'll rip your hand off." Fletch commented.

Relieved, Bob moved to the other side of the SUV and stated "Good to have you back among the living, and I wouldn't think of it. I have better plans for my appendages than coddling you." They looked at each other, got in and slammed their respective doors. Fastening his seat belt Bob jammed the key in the ignition and demanded, "I want to know about this new lady in your life and I'm going to keep driving you all over Washington DC until I get the whole story."

"Is that a threat?" Fletch asked, locking his own seat belt into place.

"You bet your proverbial bippie it is." Bob slammed the big black machine into reverse to prove his point. Fletch held on and started talking.

Chapter Sixteen
Homecoming

Feb. 24, 2001 / 07:50 am MST / Salt Lake City, Utah / home of F/O Kelly Hunter

"May our lives be so filled with awe that we have no time for fear."

-   Anne Wilson Schaef

The blade sang as it cut through the air in a final downward arc. Kelly breathed out and cleared her mind of everything but the dance of her body and the Katana in her hand. Light and shadow played against her closed eyelids. She was aware of the coolness of her martial arts dojo and the slight tang of the clove oil she used to polish the steel weapon. The 200-year-old Japanese sword was an extension of her arm. She stepped forward and gracefully slowed the blade, tip down at a 45-degree angle to the floor.

Kelly had practiced the IAIDO technique for "drawing the sword" hundreds of times. To perfect it would require hundreds more. The last move would have been used by a Samurai to clear the blade of excess blood after having cleanly cut down the threat. Samurai did not approve of "butchers" who could not kill mercifully with one cut. In Sun Tzu's writings on the art of war a true martial artist avoided a fight at all costs until forced into it without alternative. Then they brought it to an end. Quickly and decisively.

Kelly twisted the blade and continued the sleek motion by bringing it horizontally in front of her, handle first. She rotated the blade vertically across her left shoulder and drew it down her sleeve between her thumb and index finger. Her fingers held the opening of the scabbard at her waist and guided the blade in while sheathing it. Back straight and chin up, Kelly settled into a kneeling position as she exhaled and slid the sword smoothly into its scabbard. It locked in with a delicate "click".

Exercise completed, she opened her eyes. Kelly sat on the white Berber carpet of her practice area bathed in a beam of early morning sunlight. The Kata had ended exactly where it had begun. The room was peaceful. Light and airy with three of the four walls mirrored. Today they bounced rainbows of colored light against the floor. Serenity washed over her in a soothing wave as she brought herself back from the meditative pleasure of IAIDO.

Breathing deeply, she enjoyed a faint aroma of bacon and eggs from the breakfast that she had cooked for her son. The sounds of the birds and a new day filtered into her consciousness. Life was rich and filled with possibilities.

"Bye mom. Thanks!" Her son's voice echoed faintly down the hallway.

"Wait! Wait!" Kelly jumped to her feet feeling like a trap door spider ambushing him before he could run off without a hug. She couldn't help herself. Every minute with her son was becoming more precious and less frequent. He was growing up and she was gone too much. Placing her sword in its rack, she bowed herself out of the dojo and ran up the stairs to the laundry room. She managed to head him off before he could escape. Her lanky son gave her a hurried hug. She squeezed him back, allowing herself a brief moment to enjoy the bony warmth of her teenager. Cory endured the onslaught of maternal affection before grinning down at her and loping off for his old red pickup truck.

"Bye kiddo. Love ya," Kelly smiled.

"Love ya too mom. See you later."

She sighed and watched him disappear around the corner. Squealing tires and an engine that needed a muffler made her cringe. Kelly suspected that he liked the resulting racket. She'd have to talk to him about that because the neighbors didn't.

The phone rang. Kelly hit the garage door button and sprinted for the kitchen. Sliding to a stop at the counter, she whipped the phone to her ear. "East Valley Animal Shelter," she answered.

There was a pause. Then a clipped voice responded, "First officer Kelly Hunter?" Kelly's playful mood evaporated as soon as she recognized the baritone of her Chief Pilot Captain Ken Swift.

"Yes sir. This is she. Sorry about that Captain Swift. What can I do for you?"

"Am I right in assuming that our recent pay cuts have forced you to take a second job at the dog pound?" he asked dryly. Captain Swift had never been known for his sense of humor. Kelly was one of the few pilots who knew he even had one. He did. It was just very desiccated.

"A girl's gotta' do what a girl's gotta' do sir."

" I'm calling about the report you filed regarding the mugging on your layover. First I want to know if you're all right? Did you go to the hospital or sustain any injuries?

"I'm fine Ken. Just a few scrapes and bumps. Nothing I wouldn't get in a good sparring match. No worries about on-the-job injuries." Kelly said, boosting herself to a seat on the kitchen counter. "I was more concerned with getting a police report filed with law enforcement in Seattle."

"Your attachment indicated that you wanted me to call and talk to them instead of your filling out a standard report. Is there any particular reason for that?"

Kelly understood her Chief Pilot's brusque approach to the matter and was not intimidated. "Yes sir. I felt that you would probably have more luck in getting their attention than I would. I also think that this was more than an attempted mugging, as I stated in my report to you. This may be something that is specific to flight crews. I think they should be cautioned about it in the next air crew security bulletin we issue." Kelly had to force herself to stop here and not push her speculation further.

Let Ken ask the questions and make the decision himself. She thought. *Captain Swift backed his pilots as long as they were upfront with him.*

"Your report was quite detailed but what makes you think this attack is indicative of a broader threat to our flight crews? It happened on a layover. Not in the air."

"Several things." Kelly began. "Bear with me here. I didn't mention that the gentleman who came to my aid was a Federal

Air Marshal. He had definite concerns because the assailants had followed me from the coffee shop and waited for me until I left the museum."

"You're an attractive lady. That might have had something to do with it."

"Second." Kelly continued, brushing off the comment. "He felt that the organization of the attack and its apparent discipline indicated that they were after something other than rape or money from me. He thought they were after my ID."

"You mention here that they appeared to be of Middle Eastern origin?" the Chief pilot noted, following along on Kelly's report.

"Yes, sir." she agreed. "I know that the company frowns on racial profiling but those are just the facts. They may or may not be of importance."

"And what else concerns you about this incident?" Captain Swift prompted.

"An email I received from Henry. He's the concierge at the Mayflower Hotel in Seattle."

"Go on." Ken said.

"Henry checked with the hotel's security department and determined that pilot certificates, airline uniforms and other flight crew badges and credentials have been stolen from our layover rooms." Kelly concluded. "My own monthly bid packet disappeared from my suitcase. I'm certain I had it in there." she added defensively, taking advantage of his silence to add "This worries me. I thought you could officially notify the Seattle Police and any other Federal Agencies that you deem appropriate."

"I see your point." he allowed. "This will go in the next crew bulletin and I will forward it to our Security Department. I'll also recommend that we include this in the security alert portion of our next recurrent training classes."

"Thank you, sir." Kelly said. "Should I file the police report or will you?"

"I've already contacted the Seattle Police and spoken with some of their detectives." he admitted. "They told me they have their hands full with other local matters.

Unless you can identify these men they'll take the information and file it but take no further action."

"Well." Kelly sighed. "That went pretty much as expected."

"I think we'll be fine handing it over to Delta's Security Department." Captain Swift reassured her. "We do appreciate your heads-up for the flight crews though."

Hiding the disappointment in her voice Kelly responded "Thanks for getting back to me on it. Let me know if there's anything else I can do."

"I will. But no, I think you can leave it to the professionals now. From the looks of it you're going to have your hands full with captain training on the 767." he said. "If I were you, I'd stop worrying about this and get to work on the books. It's like having a fire hose jammed into your brain 24/7 in that school. There's lots of information and very little time to absorb it."

Kelly wedged the phone between her shoulder and ear as she grabbed a package of whole bean coffee from the cupboard and poured it into the grinder. "Good advice sir. I think I'll go do that right now."

" Best of luck. I'm sure you'll do fine. You always do." A dial tone signaled the end of the conversation. Kelly hung up feeling vaguely dissatisfied with the results. She took her frustration out on the coffee beans by grinding them noisily into a rich black powder.

Five minutes later she was sitting in front of her computer with a strong mug of the brew and looking undecidedly between the volumes of 767 manuals and the email web page with Shaheera's message on it. Before signing off Shaheera had pestered Kelly about "that fine man" she'd given her wings to. Kelly took a sip of coffee and made a face. It was way too strong. She shut down the email window, inserted a disk into 767 systems and reached for the training manual. Immersing her mind in aircraft systems was a safe-haven of sorts. At least there were predictable answers to these problems.

If Fletch wants to find me he will. she thought. "Stop it." she muttered to herself and focused on the page entitled "Boeing 767 / 300 ER hydraulic Systems".

Chapter Seventeen
Good Advice

*March 6, 2001 / 11:15 am MST / enroute /
DAL flight 1442 / SLC-PHX- JFK*

"Be realistic. Expect a miracle."

- **Ian Growler**

At 41,000 feet, the view to the South was magnificent. Everything from the layered red and gold of Zion's National Park to the deep turquoise of Lake Powell stood out in brilliant clarity. Kelly couldn't get enough of it.

"Look at that!" Captain Granger said. "I can see the curvature of the Earth! Where did all the smog go?"

Kelly peeked past the back of his head as he enjoyed the horizon to the North. He was right. It was a rare day. "Don't know. Don't care." she smiled. "This is the kind of flying I signed on for."

Kelly decided to change to the next high-altitude map and reached into her flight kit. Her hand slid into the bag between the books and closed on a folded rectangle of paper. It didn't feel like a map. She pulled it out and looked at it. Her eyes widened. The letter must have been hidden in the batch of company mail she"d tossed in two weeks ago. The envelope was addressed to "First Officer Kelly Hunter. Delta Airlines". The return address was listed as "E. Fletcher. Washington DC". Kelly glanced at Captain Granger. He was busy filing a position report. This was the slow portion of the flight to New York City. She could allow herself a quick break.

"Bill?" she said. "Would you watch the airplane and the radios for a minute? I want to read something."

"Sure." he responded, keying in a request for the East Coast weather. "I've got the aircraft and the radios." "Thanks." Kelly took out her Leatherman, flipped open the pocket knife and slid the short blade under the flap of the envelope. There was a neatly folded typewritten page inside. In the upper left-hand corner was a return address and a stylized "From the Desk of Eugene Fletcher" logo. The statement was imprinted over a lightly etched snow owl. Its wings were spread and it carried an arrow in its talons. *How appropriate.* she thought and smiled in spite of herself. Her heart warmed at his words.

"First Officer Hunter,

In all the years that I have served as a Federal Air Marshal the gift of your wings was the highest honor that I have ever been afforded. It is with deep gratitude that I accept them.

If you are ever in the Washington DC area I would like to have the opportunity to take you to dinner and personally thank you. I also have some photos I would appreciate your feedback on regarding the gentlemen that we met in the alley.

My office number is (916) 705-1323, or I can be reached on my personal cell phone at (916) 705-1337.

Sincerely,

Eugene Fletcher."

Kelly sighed. *It's strictly business. Probably better that way.* she admonished herself. She opened the envelope to return the letter. A scrap of paper with a handwritten note fluttered onto her lap. She picked it up and read the brief addendum.

"P.S. Please find any excuse that you can to have a layover in Washington DC as soon as possible. Your wings are kept close to my heart. I've never worked so hard for a dinner date in my life but I would gladly do it again. - Fletch

Kelly stared at the scrap of paper. She realized she was grinning like a Cheshire cat. *You're in trouble now.* she thought. Composing herself, she folded the papers and slipped them into her shirt pocket. "Thanks Bill. I've got the aircraft again. Did I miss anything while I was away?" she asked.

"Just a frequency switch to Denver Center." he replied. "Smooth sailing all the way to New York City where it's 42 degrees and clear. There are a few little cumulus clouds trying to turn into thunderstorms but nothing we can't dodge."

"Sounds good. I'm ready to be there."

"Me too." Bill replied as he shifted in his seat. "Are you planning on going anywhere for dinner tonight?"

"I owe Shaheera dinner for a favor she did for me." Kelly laughed. "She's kind of blackmailing me for some personal girl talk."

Bill took the hint. "I'd barge right in and invite myself along but I'll take a rain check. You two would probably gang up and embarrass the heck out of me until I left anyway." he admitted.

"Thanks Bill. You've pretty much got us pegged don't you?"

"Yup" he admitted. "I've been married long enough to know when I'm outgunned and outmatched."

A chime sounded in the cockpit and a blue light illuminated on the overhead panel. Kelly switched her headset to the interphone selection.

"Cockpit." she answered.

Shaheera's honeyed voice responded. "Hey y'all we have two leftover meals back here if you or the boss are hungry."

"What are they?" Kelley asked.

"There's a dried-out piece of chicken and the other is some kind of mystery meat with a sauce. The flight attendants don't want them so they're all yours. Can I bring you anything?"

"Gee, you make that sound irresistibly appetizing. Let me check." Kelly looked at Bill who had been listening in. He shook his head in a definitive "no" but made a drinking gesture with his thumb and little finger tipped toward his mouth. "Thanks for the offer Shaheera. I think we'll pass on the meals. A couple of bottles of water would be nice. "

"I'm saving myself for that big lobster dinner you promised and some juicy gossip tonight." Shaheera said.

"So am I." Kelly agreed. "Dress Warm. It's cold and clear. I know just the restaurant to go to on the Hudson River."

"You got it girl." the voice responded. "I'll be right up with your drinks."

Kelly switched back to Denver Center and knew this would be an expensive girl's night out.

Kelly greased her landings on when she was in a good mood. Four hours later the passengers weren't even aware that they'd touched down at JFK International Airport.

Shaheera's bright smile was bigger than usual as she said goodbye to the people filing past the galley. The extroverted flight attendant liked nothing better than prying confidences out of her friend. Kelly had been tight-lipped about the Air Marshal. That made it all-the-more titillating to her outrageous friend.

Kelly caught Shaheera's eye as they walked down the jetway. "Judging by that smug expression I'd say the lobster isn't the only thing that's going to get a good grilling tonight." Kelly commented. Glancing behind them at the rest of the flight crew she added. "Can we wait until dinner to talk about my personal life?"

Shaheera nodded and made a lip-zipping motion with her hand. "My lips are sealed all the way to the hotel. Then you're mine. 1'll just add a nice glass of white wine to that lobster you owe me."

"Good grief Shaheera." Kelly protested. "Any more favors from you and I'll have to upgrade to captain just to pay you hush money! By the way. I did take a captain bid."

Shaheera let out an unladylike whoop. "You go girl! I mean Captain Hunter!" she squealed. "Don't think you can change the subject either." Shaheera added. "You know who I want to hear about." Kelly found herself looking forward to sharing the good news in the misplaced letter.

True to her word Shaheera behaved herself all the way to the hotel. "I'll give you half an hour to get ready. Then I'll meet you in the lobby." she said as Kelly stepped out of the elevator. Kelly grinned and waved a quick goodbye at the closing doors. Her room was just a few steps away. She opened her door, put her bags down and pulled off her boots.

Leaping onto the bed Kelly propped her head comfortably on the double-stacked pillows and pulled Fletcher's note from her pocket. Reading it again made her smile.

An hour later the sunset painted a deep lavender outline of the World Trade Center on Manhattan's twinkling skyline. The last rays edged it all in gold. Shaheera peered at Kelly over the rim of her glass of white wine.

"So, how much longer do I have to wait before you tell me about this Air Marshal and why you gave him your wings?" she asked. "I know you're not the ice queen you'd like people to think you are." Shaheera smiled and allowed her friend a quiet moment as they watched lights come on aboard barges on the Hudson River. Taking a sip of her Coke and lime, Kelly turned back to her ebony-eyed interrogator.

"It's a long story and I know you don't want the Reader's Digest version."

Shaheera cupped her chin in her hands. "I have all night." she replied. "Have you seen him again?" she asked. "Did he track you down yet?"

"Whoa girl." Kelly laughed. "All in good time. I think you'll enjoy the real story much more than anything you've managed to cook up in that romance-riddled mind of yours."

"I doubt that." Shaheera chuckled. "I have a fantastic imagination. But you go right ahead and give it your best shot. I'll order another wine." She angled a coquettish glance at a young waiter on his way to another table and waved a slender hand at him.

"Oh, sir." she beckoned. "Would you please bring me another white Zinfandel?"

The twenty-something server had never been addressed as "sir" before. That and the combination of Kelly's long-legged golden beauty and Shaheera's dark exotic looks were too much for him. His head swiveled and stuck in their direction while his body continued on course.

"Look out!" Another waiter swerved around him, narrowly missing the smitten man's tray. Drinks sloshed as their waiter juggled the contents back into submission, regained his composure and reassured Shaheera. "Yes ma'am! One white Zinfandel coming right up." He hesitated, stared and smiled nervously at her.

"I'll be right back with that white Zinfandel." He headed for the bar, remembered his original mission at the other table, and turned around narrowly missing the other waiter again.

Shaheera giggled demurely.

"You ought to be ashamed of yourself." Kelly said. "You did that on purpose!"

"On the contrary." Shaheera said. "WE did that. You never did have any idea of the effect you have on men. It's like you're wearing blinders." She took another sip of wine. "I'm getting bored again. Unless you want me to do something else shameless you'd better start entertaining me."

"It was a dark and stormy night!" Kelly blathered, feigning panic.

Shaheera wagged a warning finger at her.

"No." Kelly protested. "It really was a dark and stormy night. We were flying into hurricane grade winds, turbulence and ice in Seattle of all places. I met Fletcher on the layover." She smiled at the memory. "I think he saved my life."

Shaheera's dark eyes grew large as she slid closer to the edge of her seat. "Now that's what I'm talking about!" she breathed, hand at her throat. "You have the best things happen to you. Why don't those things happen to me?"

Kelly blinked in exasperation. "It wasn't exactly one of your bodice-ripping fantasies Shaheera. If you don't mind being followed and attacked by a group of angry Middle Eastern men, you too can hope for a white knight to come flying through the fog to your rescue. Now hush and I'll tell you all about it."

Shaheera actually did hush, which was a rare occurrence in her personable life. She accepted her second glass of wine from the waiter with barely a glance in his direction and listened to Kelly's story with focused intensity.

The dusky beauty of her features registered shock and indignation when Kelly described the battle in the alley. A dreamy look softened it as Kelly described Fletcher. She showed a great deal more frustration on learning that Kelly left Fletch without exchanging phone numbers.

"Good Lord Girl!" she exclaimed in agitation. "How many times does the poor man have to throw himself at your feet before you take the hint?" She crossed her arms in vexation. "If I hadn't told him I thought you wanted his body he'd probably think you weren't interested at all!"

Kelly's jaw dropped in disbelief.

Shaheera's hands flew to her mouth, eyes wide. "Oops." she offered lamely.

Kelly dropped her face into her hands. "Shaheera, please tell me you didn't do that."

The unrepentant flight attendant grinned. "Well, he seemed pleased at the prospect and someone has to do your flirting for you."

Kelly groaned.

"You just try and tell me you don't want him." Shaheera studied her friend's heated complexion and proclaimed "Hah! See. It's obvious. Have you heard from him?"

Kelly glared at her friend and nodded.

"Well then Captain Hunter, I think that I might have rescued you from yourself and missing out on something wonderful. As your advisor in matters of the heart I want you to know that regardless of your black belt I will personally kick your Scandinavian butt if you don't follow up on this one." Shaheera deftly cracked another lobster claw, dipped it in butter and added "So when does he want to see you again and what do you intend to do about it?"

Biting into the succulent meat with relish, she thoroughly enjoyed the parade of emotions marching across Kelly's features.

"He said that he wants to see me as soon as possible to look at some photographs of suspects."

Shaheera stopped in mid-chew. "And..." she prompted.

Kelly's face lit up with a wide smile.

"And he says that he wants to have dinner with me. I think I'd like that very much," she added. "Damn, I hate it when you're always right about me." she laughed. "Thank you."

"Damn right I am and you're welcome," Shaheera replied graciously, wiping her fingers on a napkin. "Now what are you going to do about it?" she persisted.

"Um, call and accept?" Kelly replied uncertainly.

Shaheera rolled her eyes.

"If that gorgeous man ever manages to get you out there you tell him that HE owes me a dinner." She pointed a finger threateningly at Kelly. "And so do you. Again."

She ripped the other claw off and cracked it, muttering under her breath. "I can't afford to keep doing favors for you two or I'm going to have to go on a diet."

Chapter Eighteen
Passion and Reason

March 10, 2001 / 09:58 am EST /
Washington, DC

**"*Reason, ruling alone, is a force confining,
and passion unattended, is a flame that
burns to its own destruction.*"**

-   Khalil Gibran

The nation's capital had been suffering from weeks of unyielding rain. Fletch's mood was deteriorating along with the weather. It had been three weeks since he'd sent Kelly the letter. There had been no response. He worried about Kelly and he worried about his agreement to keep her in the dark. Guilt mixed with unfulfilled desire was a depressing cocktail. *Maybe he didn't deserve a reply.* He thought miserably.

A cheerful ray of sunlight peeked under his curtains. He glowered at the invasive little beam and debated whether he should get up and open the drapes or continue to sulk in the dark at his desk. The mental image of himself sitting in a funk suddenly struck him as funny and a tad melodramatic. *I was never very good at being pathetic.* he thought. Fletch looked at the target on the wall and felt compelled to get his bow. *That's a good sign.* he realized. *Maybe there's hope for me.*

Pushing away from the unfinished paperwork, he walked to a quiver of arrows hanging on the wall and secured it to its belt. Then he took the recurve bow off its hook. His gaze was drawn by a glimmer of gold reflected in the mirror. Kelly's wings were still sitting on his nightstand. He couldn't bring himself to put them away. His heart hurt. He reached for them, hesitated, and turned back to the target.

Nocking the arrow into the slot on the bowstring Fletch wondered if he should let someone else take Kelly's case. Personal hopes aside, he worried that she was still in danger and he was no closer to finding Atta.

If she'd wanted anything to do with you she would have gotten back to you by now. he told himself sternly. *Don't be a pest!*

He wondered if he'd just imagined the attraction between them. *Get a grip*. he admonished himself, breathing in and raising the bow to his eye level. *She's an Airline Pilot and probably has millionaires and celebrities trying to date her. You're just an Air Marshal living on a government salary.*

Fletch relaxed, breathed out slowly and pictured the arrow in the center of the target, and the target being a spot between the eyes of Mohammed Atta. Leaning slightly into the draw, he let his fingers relax and released the arrow. He held the position until a rewarding "thunk" announced a hit. The shaft quivered satisfyingly in the middle of the red dot. Fletch stood up and smiled, studying the results of his shot. Instinctive archery was his drug of choice. It drowned his worries and calmed his restless mind.

He slid the second arrow out of his quiver. Fitting it to the bow and raising it to the target. *She was just being polite*. he thought. *Didn't her constant disappearing act give you a hint?*

Fletch drew the bowstring to the corner of his mouth and prepared to let go. His fingers began to release tension on the shaft. The phone rang. Fletch couldn't stop the final escape of the arrow. A sharp "crack" announced its arrival. The shaft splintered as the head hit a nail at the edge of the target and buried itself in the drywall.

Fletch stared at the dart in frustration and stormed over to the phone. Bow gripped tightly in one hand, he swept the offending handset up to his ear and growled, "Agent Fletcher – Speak!" There was a maddening silence on the other end. Fletch rolled his eyes to the ceiling in exasperation, asking God to give him patience. He glared at the phone and repeated more gently "Agent Eugene Fletcher here. Hello?"

A feminine voice composed itself and responded. "Agent Fletcher? This is Kelly. That is, First Officer Kelly Hunter." It was Fletch's turn to be struck silent. Kelly had to prompt him back to reality.

"Fletch? Did I call at a bad time?"

"No." he continued more softly. "No Kelly. Not at all. I was just poking holes in my wall. I'm happy to hear from you."

"I'm sorry it took so long to get back to you" she said. "I didn't find your letter in my flight kit until two days ago. I'm afraid I owe you an apology." Her words spilled out in a rush.

"Not a problem." Fletch reassured her. "Right about now the only thing that would upset me is if you hung up."

If Kelly had any doubts about Fletch's interest in her they fled with his admission. She breathed a sigh of relief.

"I'm glad to hear that." she stated. "I called to say that I would be happy to take you up on your dinner invitation and look at the photos you have." She cringed inwardly, knowing that she'd been holding the business aspect out like a shield or a wall between them.

"Dinner would be great and I'll bring the photos as well." he stated, sounding more guarded.

Kelly heard the uncertainty in his voice. It touched her heart. She realized he was just as vulnerable as she was. "I'm not very good at this." she ventured. "What I'm trying to say is, it's you I want to see. The photos are a good excuse for me." There was a gentle exhalation on the other end of the line. It sounded like he had been holding his breath for weeks.

"Not a bad recovery for someone who's not very good at this." he chuckled. "Neither am I. When are you coming out and when are you going to run away again?" The sound of Kelly's laughter flowed over him. It felt good.

"I don't plan on running away this time Fletch." He could almost hear her smiling. "If you know what's good for you, you'll be planning your own escape." she laughed. "I take no prisoners."

"Well ma'am." Fletch affected a Texas twang. "I always have an escape route. In your case I'd happily surrender if I knew when your next layover here would be. I'll even wash my white flag for the occasion."

"Unfortunately, it may be awhile before I can get out there on a layover." she said. "I just finished my last trip as a co-pilot yesterday. I start a six-week 767/757 captain upgrade training course in Atlanta on the 15th."

"Oh." Fletch sounded like he was just starting down the other side of the emotional roller coaster.

"However." Kelly continued. "In the interest of National Security and identifying the bad guys I'd like to find a hotel where I can stay and visit you for a couple of days between now and then."

Fletch was dumbfounded.

"That would be wonderful." he said. He felt like he had been tracking an elusive puma for weeks only to find her purring contentedly and curled up at his side. Kelly was fighting to keep the habitual walls firmly lowered and not go all professional on him again. The idea of losing this opportunity scared her more than what Fletch or anyone else might think.

"I want to spend some time getting to know you Fletch. We've already tried the hit-and-run   ships-passing-in-the-night approach." she said. "I don't know about you but I thought it left a lot to be desired."

Fletch stood grinning at the wall and holding the handset pressed to his ear. "That's putting it mildly." he replied. He decided to curb his enthusiasm. *Don't scare her off before she even gets on the plane.* he cautioned himself. *Take it slow.*

"I'd be happy to show you around D.C. for a couple of days. I'm a darn good cook. We can have a meal here or we could go out to eat. I know a few excellent restaurants in Georgetown. We can go bow-shooting if you'd like. There's an archery range a few minutes away. When can you be here?"

Fletch grimaced. *That was NOT playing it cool.* he told himself. *So much for not scaring her off.* He realized he'd been looking forward to sharing everything he enjoyed with her. To his relief, Kelly laughed again. He loved her laugh. It was smooth and comfortable. "I think a restaurant will be fine for now." she reassured him. "I just want to enjoy your company. I'd like for you to be able to relax too." she added. The truth be known, Kelly was afraid of what might happen if she had dinner at Fletcher's apartment. She'd dreamt about him too often to fool herself about her feelings. As self-assured as he seemed, Kelly liked his boyish enthusiasm and the fact that he was a bit flustered. It was endearing. She looked at her calendar.

"How about Tuesday?" she asked. "That's the day after tomorrow. Does that work for you?"

Fletch dug through the papers on his desk until he found his work schedule. It listed a trip assignment for him starting Wednesday morning. *"No" wasn't an option. He'd find a way.*

"Perfect." Fletch said. "That works for me."

"I guess it's meant to be when it comes together that easily." Kelly said. "I'll book a hotel and get myself on a flight to

Washington National on Tuesday morning. I'm glad it worked out."

"Sounds like a plan." Fletch grinned. "Call me back with the arrival time and flight number." He felt a wave of relief sweep over him and added "Kelly. I'm looking forward to seeing you."

"I'll call you." she assured him. It felt good to say "I'm looking forward to seeing you again too Fletch."

"Talk to you soon then." he said.

"Bye." she replied. She stood holding the phone and waiting for him to hang up. They both realized that neither of them wanted to be the first to let go and hung up simultaneously.

Fletch stood with his bow in one hand and a smile on his face. He looked up and thought *Thank you Great Spirit. If you're going to answer all of my prayers today maybe I'd better make a list.* The small beam of sunlight had crept further into Fletch's room. It reflected sparks of gold from the wings on his nightstand. Fletch took this as an answer.

Two thousand miles west of Washington DC Kelly stood beside her home computer. She was vacillating between panic and being thrilled. Catching a glimpse of her own panicked expression mirrored in the window, she burst out laughing.

"So, Captain Hunter." she mocked her reflection. "You can fight your way through engine fires, thunderstorms and roving bands of Middle Eastern muggers but you're going to let an Air Marshal scare you?" She put her hands on her hips and gave her twin image a disapproving scowl. It scowled back. "Well." she told it. "You've got to admit he's one very attractive Air Marshal." The reflection grinned back and gave no sign of disagreeing with Kelly's opinion.

"All right then." she ordered herself. "Get those flight times and stop looking so panicked."

"Hey Mom. Who ya' talking to?" her son's voice asked. She looked up to find a freckled face grinning at her from the doorway.

"I, um. You know what? You're way too mature for your age." she recovered. "By the way how did that math test go?" she asked. The face dissolved in a flurry of clomping size twelve sneakers and trailing excuses about having to go to soccer practice. Kelly smiled and sat down to list herself on a flight.

Chapter Nineteen
Sanctuary

March 12, 2001 / 5:52 pm EST / Washington National Airport, Washington, DC

"Surrender your fears and you will know peace. That is knowing your place in the universe, and the perfection of your imperfect journey."

- **V. Walker – Author**

Her flight was dodging closely spaced restricted areas including the White House and the Pentagon. The step-down altitudes and airspeeds had to be perfectly timed. Any deviation could have serious consequences – like getting shot down.

Kelly sat in the passenger cabin and traced the flight path in her mind. She'd flown this route many times. *Right about now..* she predicted, *the pilot will crank in a hard right bank and throw out the gear and flaps.* The big jet rolled to the right on cue. A rumble of gear and flaps dropping pleased her. *Good job guys.* she thought, trying not to be too smug about her accuracy.

Kelley looked down at the Key Bridge and wondered if Fletch was on it. A warm glow rippled across her. She'd be seeing him again in minutes and she was a nervous wreck. Back seat flying the approach to Washington National Airport was her way of calming down. The rest of the four-hour flight had her recalling the texture of Fletch's skin, his touch, the way he looked at her. She couldn't help herself. *Just have a nice dinner and look at the photos.* she told herself. *Why are you so nervous? Why are you so happy?*

Fletch stood beside the large picture window at the gate where Kelly's flight would be arriving. His restless anticipation convinced him to wait at the airport. He'd been there an hour. The target in his apartment was confetti. Shredded by his vain attempts to relax. He looked to the North and squinted into the glare of landing lights. The beam illuminated water droplets as the nose of a 757 appeared in a halo of late afternoon drizzle. Rolling out of a steep bank, the plane leveled its wings and plunked firmly onto the runway in a roar of spray and thrust reversers.

That has to be Kelly's flight. he thought. Much to his dismay he found his heart racing. He couldn't keep a straight thought in his head and it occurred to him that he had no idea what to say to her when she got off the plane. The shoulder holster he always wore kept his Sig Sauer comfortingly tucked against his body. His customary combat knife was secured in his boot. They were no comfort to him in this situation.

Give me an honest battle with the bad guys and I'd know what to do. he worried. *Give me a beautiful woman who haunts my soul and I'm toast.* Fletch felt defenseless. He had to remind himself that Kelly was coming because she wanted to be with him. That thought didn't help either. It made his knees weak and only served to worsen his condition. *Just have a nice dinner together and go over the photos.* he thought reasonably. *Enjoy the time you can share with Kelly and be grateful for whatever comes of it. Even if it's just friendship.* He hoped for more but would settle for less to be with her.

The 757 nosed into the gate and shut its engines down. Passengers began to spill out of the doors and into the arms of friends and loved ones. Fletch craned his neck searching for a head of long silvery hair. Kelley's eyes found his first. The smile that lit her face when she saw him blinded him to anything else. She hurried toward him. Without thinking, he reached out and took her hand, pulling her close. Without resisting, she threw her arms around him. Standing quietly together with the crowd spilling around them the world seemed to stop. All that existed was the "rightness" of that moment.

"Fletch?

"What?" he murmured into her hair.

"You're even more gorgeous than I remembered. I just wanted to make sure it was you. That is you, isn't it?" Kelly whispered mischievously. It was true. She felt audacious saying it. She was surprised to see him redden and grin, apparently at a loss for words. He looked away for a moment, then he took her bags and her hand and led her toward his car.

"Yes it's me." he said simply. Halfway there he turned and looked at her, afraid she'd disappear. He circled his arm protectively around her waist and favored her with a glance that would have melted titanium.

"Kelly..."

"What?"

"Thank you for coming. The look in his eyes said it all.

"Thank you for giving me reason to." Kelly responded. *Fletcher has a spirit that deserves to be cherished. Just like he does.* She thought, making a vow to herself to do just that. Kelly smiled and followed him to his car.

The drive to her hotel was filled with light talk about the rainy weather and what restaurants to consider for dinner. "When would you like me to look through the photos of your suspects?" Kelley asked. So far they'd managed to keep the conversation businesslike. They were both more comfortable with that. The intimate confines of the car seemed to intensify their awareness of each other and it made them nervous.

"I have them in the car." Fletch said. "We could look at them after you check in or later after dinner."

"Where should we go over them?" Kelly asked. "Are they classified?"

"Yes they are." Fletch replied, taking the exit marked "Pentagon". "Your room would be fine or we could go to my place." An awkward silence filled the car as the ramifications of being alone together became clear. They had arrived at the Hotel. Fletch found a space and parked. He got out and opened the door for Kelly.

She stepped out and stood facing him, afraid to look up. He didn't move. She could feel the heat from his body and the need in her own. He took her chin gently in his hands and tilted her face toward him. Kelley kept her eyes down knowing that if she looked, she was lost.

"Kelly." Fletch whispered. "May I kiss you?" She looked up and fell into those smoldering deep blue eyes. The need, the desire in them was so great that she fell willingly. Thankfully.

"Yes." she wanted to beg. "Yes, please."

She closed her eyes and heard him whisper "please." echoing her own thoughts just before his lips touched hers. Gently at first. Seeking permission. He tasted like the sky after a thunderstorm and she drank him in.

He wrapped his arms around her and pressed her against the car probing more deeply, enveloping her mouth with his. Cradling her head in his hand. She melted into him letting her hands explore the lean hard muscles of his back and trace the lines of his waist as his were tracing the firm slim stretches of hers.

Kelly could hardly breathe. She didn't care. If her wildly beating heart stopped and she died. She didn't care. Fletch couldn't believe what he was doing. He couldn't believe Kelly's response. *This striking controlled Airline Pilot was losing it because of him. The feel of her body melting against his and her mouth so eagerly matching his passion with hers was too much.*

Fletch prided himself on his own self-restraint and it was going fast. He couldn't think. Desperately indulging himself in one last long lingering moment, he forced himself to step back. He held Kelly at arm's length. Studying her. Her eyes were still closed and her breath was coming in gasps. She looked ravished. Tendrils of hair had escaped their restraints and framed her face in a halo of light. Her cheeks were flushed. He thought she was the most beautiful thing he'd ever seen.

Fletch spoke, unthinking, as soon as he could slow his own breathing.

"Can we go to your room?" Kelly's eyes snapped open. He was horrified at his own words. "That was presumptuous of me." he apologized. "I'm sorry."

He watched fearfully as an unreadable flash of consideration passed behind her eyes. *What have I done?* he asked himself painfully.

Kelly's first impulse was to *"do the right thing"* as her instinct to conform to society's dictates required. *She should tell him no and go to her room alone. She should not be that easy to get.* That thought left her feeling devastated and hypocritical.

She looked into Fletch's eyes and saw the concern there. The unnecessary shame. At that moment all of her fears dropped away. The impulse to explain herself, to let him know that he was her first in years seemed trite and tawdry. Either Fletch knew her as she was or he didn't. She didn't want to play games.

"I don't want to eat." she said. Suddenly calm. "I'm not hungry or thirsty or tired. All I want is you and I can't wait any longer." She smiled into his astonished face. "I think we both knew that when I came here."

The relief in Fletch was palpable. A weight seemed to lift from his shoulders. He would have carried her to her room if she hadn't grabbed his hand and pulled him along behind her. Checking in was a blur. Neither one of them remembered how they got through the door. All Kelly knew was that this was a gift that she gave to herself and to Fletcher and she would have no regrets. The click of the door as its lock fell into place was an invitation to paradise they both accepted.

Years of self-denial, pain and doubt fell away as Fletch took Kelly in his arms and covered her with deep probing kisses.

The sun had gone down hours ago. They'd never made it to dinner. Their hunger for each other had been more demanding. Exhausted, Kelley pulled Fletch to her. He sank into her arms. When he kissed her she could taste herself, sweet and salty on his lips. They lay in a happy tangle of each other's arms and legs. Spent, satisfied and safe. Their bodies fitting together like pieces in a puzzle.

"Just let me die here and now." Kelly spoke softly. "It doesn't get any better than this." She smiled a tiny happy smile and nuzzled into his chest. Her eyes closed and she slipped into the sweet and untroubled slumber of a child. Fletch looked down at Kelly and wrapped his arms comfortably around her. He wondered how he'd managed to end up in this most hoped-for and hopeless of situations. Tilting his head and resting his cheek on her hair, he decided to forego thinking for a while and enjoy their small perfect sanctuary. He drifted off to sleep listening to the lullaby of her heartbeat.

They awoke hours later and couldn't make it out of bed. "I should get you some food," Fletch managed to say. "I just don't want you to stop what you're doing." he gasped. "I don't want to let you go." Kelly ran her mouth along his chest and murmured, "I love the taste and feel of you." Her hands caressed him. "I enjoy the exploration. It excites me." Fletch closed his eyes and lost control.

He fell back totally spent and marveled as she sat up with a cat-who-ate-the-canary grin and a sultry look in her eyes. "You really do like that don't you?" he gasped weakly.

Kelly licked her lips and dabbed primly at the corner of her mouth with the tip of the sheet. "Yep." she declared. He would've laughed if he'd had any breath left in him.

"Oh Lord I think I'm in trouble!" was all he said, and he was right. They fell asleep again with the rain pattering softly against the window, locked in each other's arms.

Kelly stretched luxuriously and scooted closer to the warmth spooned against her back. She was in Washington, and the warm body wasn't a dream. It was Fletch. His soft snoring sounded like the purring of a big cat. His hand cupped her breast. She smiled and placed her hand over his. A dim light crept into the room as she turned her head to look at him. She rested her cheek on his arm. Fletch's face was framed against the white linen of the pillow. The dark strands of his hair mingled with the silver gold of hers like moonlight and shadows. His fine strong features were softened by the sensual curve of his lips.

Kelly noticed that the aggressive arch of his eyebrows, so much like the wings of a hawk in wakeful vigilance, had relaxed in sleep. *There was,* she thought, *if not entirely an innocence about him at least a less serious expression.* She rolled over and propped her chin in her hand, studying him as if this might be her last opportunity to secure him in her memory. She hoped not but life had taught her that nothing was ever a certainty.

You take the miracles that life offers. You give thanks for them and you store the memories in a safe place. she thought. *Later, when you find yourself seeking answers. Reasons why you go on and life is still beautiful, you open that treasure chest. You take out a jewel like this and hold it up to the light.*

Sliding quietly off the bed she walked over to the window and stood on tiptoe to open the heavy drapes, leaving the gauzy ones in place. "Beautiful." She heard the simple statement and turned to see Fletch propped on one hand admiring her silhouette. He was storing jewels of his own.

She started toward him. He leapt from the bed and made for the shower. "Oh no you don't missy." he chided her. "Much as I'd like to, if we don't get something to eat they'll find us both dead of exhaustion and starvation in here tomorrow." He slammed the bathroom door. She laughed thankfully.

"So. What does a girl have to do to get you to show her those pictures of the bad guys?" she called after him.

Chapter Twenty
A Tangled Web

March 14, 2001 / 10:02 am EST /
Washington, DC

"Life is what happens while you're making other plans."

- TBF

"Mmm, you taste like Juevos Rancheros." Kelly commented. Her kiss made his favorite breakfast even more enjoyable. He'd never been more at peace than he was at this moment.

Lieutenant Colonel Joe Johnson would not approve. a voice nagged at the back of his mind. His brow furrowed for a moment as he considered that unpleasant possibility. Straightening his shoulders he shrugged it off. *Joe has nothing to do with it.* he told himself. *This is my private life. I haven't done anything wrong.* He looked up.

"You sure you know what you're doing hanging out with an old 'bullet flinger' like me?" he asked impulsively. "You could be on a yacht in the Mediterranean with a prince or a CEO right now if you wanted to."

"Where did that come from?" Kelly laughed. "You're not trying to get rid of me are you?"

"No." Fletch declared, looking distraught and wondering why he'd asked.

"I guess I could at that." she agreed. "Personally." she continued, grasping his shirt and pulling him toward her. "I think I'm far too good for that. I deserve nothing less than being right here with a magnificent old bullet flinger like you". He brushed a strand of hair from her face and returned a lopsided grin. The effect she was having on him made him feel happily stupid.

"Stop that and eat." he said. Pointing to her half-finished plate. You'll need to keep your strength up. We still have all day and you're bringing out my amorous side again". Kelly grinned and finished her meal. She was Looking forward to spending the rest of the day with Fletcher and seeing if she recognized any of her assailants. She hoped it would clear up some disturbing questions that had been nagging her. They paid and drove to Fletcher's assigned living quarters.

Kelly walked into Fletcher's apartment and gave it an appraising look. He closed the door behind them. The place was simple and without artifice. It held a few unique items that had meaning for him. Her wings sat on his nightstand. She approved. When Fletch slid his arms around her it brought back a flood of erotic memories. She melted into his embrace before giving him a knowing look and placing a hand on his chest.

"As a wise man told me earlier today. Oh no you don't mister. As much as I'd love to, not until we look at those mug shots."

Fletch feigned a sad-eyed look of utter dejection. "I forgot to tell you that I don't take rejection well. You're right. Photo identification first. Then the instinctive archery lesson I promised." He gave her a hopeful look. "If I'm lucky I might get taken advantage of again later?"

"I'd say you're a very lucky guy," Kelly reassured him. "You're lucky I have such remarkable self-control." Fletch grinned. anticipating his good fortune. He picked up his briefcase and set it on the table. Placing his fingers on the latch buttons, he spun the coded locks. The top swung open and he pulled out the file.

Kelly was exploring the far end of his Spartan living quarters. "What's that thing?" Kelly asked. Surveying the shredded piece of painted padding on his wall. Fletch looked up when he saw where she was pointing.

"That's my target." he said. "I pick up my bow and shoot an arrow whenever I come in the door.

"But there are so many holes in it you can't even see the bulls-eye and it's tiny. Don't you ever put a new one up?"

"That is a new one." Fletch said. "I was a little nervous before I came to pick you up. Archery calms me down."

"And I thought I was a bundle of nerves." she laughed. Kelly walked over to the target and put a finger into the hole in the wall. "I take it you don't often miss your mark. What happened here?"

"That one's your fault." he said. "You have the dubious distinction of being able to break my concentration with a phone call."

She turned and gave him a wicked grin. "I think I'm kind of proud of that."

"All right, miss special," Fletch said. "Come over here where the light's better and place your very special behind in this chair. We have some bad guys to look at. Then we'll go have fun at the archery range." He flipped open the cover of the portfolio to reveal the same set of faces he'd seen in the TTIC database. The information posted underneath them was gone but their names were still there.

Kelly leaned forward and scrutinized them.

"Just relax. Take your time and tell me if anything jumps out at you." Fletch advised. He stifled a chuckle when he saw the intense concentration she was expending on the search. "Don't think so much. Your mind will pick out the reality better if you don't confuse it with preconceived notions. Trust your intuition."

"Thanks." she said, taking a deep breath. "Good advice. I should know that." Kelly relaxed and let her gaze flow easily over the catalog of swarthy visages. Fletch watched with interest when she selected the page with Mohamed Atta's rigid features. He thought he saw a glimmer of recognition and asked, "Did you see someone?" A moment of confusion seemed to pass as she stared at the photo. He could see the wheels turning as she sought to rationalize her reaction.

"No." Kelly replied. "I thought I did but it was just something about the eyes." She shook off the feeling and concluded "I probably had a nightmare about an expression like that."

There's such a thing as being too logical for your own good. he thought. His training had taught him not to interfere with a witness's identification process so he said nothing.

Kelly turned the page and almost jumped out of her chair in excitement. She jabbed a finger at a pockmarked face. "Now this guy I recognize." she said. "He was in the coffee shop in Seattle. I laid him flat when he attacked me in the alley!"

Fletch noted her feral expression. "Why Kelly. I do believe you enjoyed doing that." They shared a moment of mutual understanding and two predatory grins before turning back to the document. "This one goes by the name of Wail." he said. "He's used a variety of last names." Fletch caught himself before he told her about Atta, the cell and his fears about her involvement. He'd been thinking of her more as a partner than a resource. The inner struggle had taken a second too long. Kelly looked at him quizzically, as if expecting him to continue.

"Let's move on and see if you can find anyone else." he suggested. To his relief, she seemed to accept this and turned her attention back to the pages. By the third page her eyes widened in excitement. She recognized the last man on the list.

"Here's another one. This is the man who came at me from the other end of the alley. I was in real trouble before you flew out of the fog and tackled him." She tilted her head to look at Fletch. "I kind of liked that." He growled in agreement. Kelly commented "I thought you'd pick him out too. Isn't he the guy who kept running into that bruised fist of yours?" She looked down at the name. "Rasheed al... I can't pronounce it." She struggled with the foreign syllables.

"They all use several names or combinations of them." Fletch explained. "It's different in the Middle East. These guys are constantly moving around under assumed identities and slightly altered passports."

Understanding crossed her features. Kelly turned away from the folder and focused her attention on Fletch. "What's really going on here?" she asked. "These are all Middle Eastern men who change their names as they move around, apparently in and out of the country on a regular basis. If they do that in groups and have the money to finance this sort of travel, they're obviously not in it just to mug strangers." She waited.

A small worry line etching her brow. "What's going on Fletch? Why did they pick me?"

Knowing Kelly, he wasn't surprised to find she'd pretty much figured it out. He looked into her eyes and made a decision. "I'm not going to lie to you Kelly. At the risk of sounding like a bad spy movie, you've already guessed too much. You'll just have to trust me on this." He searched her face and found it still open to suggestion. She looked like she thought he might be leading up to the punch line of a bad joke.

"As you've already noted," he continued, "these people aren't your everyday criminals. We're looking for them for reasons of National Security." he informed her, caught between his feelings of loyalty to both Kelly and his profession. He hoped he hadn't crossed the line between either.

"Should I be worried?" Kelly asked. "Am I involved in something that I should know about or report to my airline?"

Fletch was being squeezed into a corner. He had to admit that in her place, he would have asked the same questions.

"That's where the trust me thing has to come into play." Fletch searched for an appropriate comparison. "You're an excellent pilot Kelly. I'd confidently fly through anything if you were at the controls. By the same token" he continued "You're smart enough to understand when I say that I can't legally tell you more. You can't even suggest what you might suspect to your airline or anyone else at this stage without jeopardizing our chances of catching these guys."

Kelly looked alarmed at the turn this had taken but seemed to accept it. The color of Fletch's eyes deepened to a midnight blue. His dark brows drew together in determination. "I hope you know I'll never let anything bad happen to you." he added. "I'm very good at my job and I do have a personal stake in seeing that you live a long, happy and lustful life." Fletch was relieved at his own off-the-wall comment and happy to see that Kelly responded to the humor in it.

"Stop looking so anxious Fletcher." she smiled. It's in my best interests to keep you trapped in the throes of desire for a long, long time. As one Sheep dog to another it's in our nature to protect and serve others. It's who we are and we do it well. I trust you."

Fletch half laughed and half felt guilty. He wondered how Kelly would feel if she knew she was being used as bait. Banishing that thought from his mind, he silently made a promise. *By my life or by my death I will protect you.* he vowed.

Fletch expected to have to do more convincing at a dear cost to his own sense of ethics and self-worth. Kelly had managed to put the whole situation into a simple and acceptable format. He felt relieved and just a little unsettled at how deeply she was able to see into his heart. "Thank you." he said. "I guess I don't have to make my case. You seem to be doing a much better job of making it for me."

She smiled, pleased at the compliment. "You're welcome. Are there any more photos to be looked at or discussions to be had before we go shoot some arrows? Can we please go play now?" she added.

"Nope. Nothing more to do here that I can't handle." Fletch said, taking the file from her and replacing it in the briefcase. "Uncle Sam and I thank you. I just have one last request before we go" he said.

"What's that?" Kelly asked.

"Please try not to outshoot me. I have that fragile male ego to deal with and I might not be able to recover from that one." Fletch said.

Two hours later he stood to her right at the archery range. She drew the bowstring back for the last time. The stiff leather of her arm guard and the bow string had found it's way underneath. It chaffed her skin, but she ignored it. Her other arrows were concentrated below and to the left of center.

"Nice grouping." he told her. Fletch had already "killed" his targets a dozen times over and was more impressed with Kelly's progress than she was. "Breathe out. let go and follow through." he coached. "Let it all go in one smooth motion." Kelly blanked her mind and did as he said. She leaned into the target and willed the arrow to be there. Seeing it as if it already was. Nothing else existed outside of the red spot in the center.

Fletch winced as he saw the long purple bruise forming on her arm where string had found its way beneath the leather arm guard. *That's got to hurt.* he thought. *Every archer has to sport a "bow kiss" eventually.* He knew she'd wear it like a Hessian's saber scar. It was Kelly's vulnerability and joyful determination that touched him.

She was more human. More real and easier to love with imperfections.

The arrow sizzled out of the bowstring and hit the target. Pinning itself dead center into the bull's eye. Kelly's whoop of glee resurrected their memorable afternoon. He couldn't help but let out a whoop of his own and accept her enthusiastic hug.

"Thank you." Kelly placed her hands together and bowed. "This unworthy student asks how I may serve the Golden Master of the Shredded Target in return for such knowledge." Fletch picked up on his role without hesitation.

"I have a very good idea of how such payment may be made 'O unworthy student of the unscathed target." Kelly grinned and ran to extract the arrows from the targets. That idea turned into a very good afternoon. The afternoon passed into early evening too quickly for either of them.

"I think I hate this part." Fletch said, gathering her to his chest as they lay entwined under the sheets. "I've got to get you out of here or you'll miss your plane and I don't want to let you go."

"I hate it too." Kelly responded truthfully. She tucked her nose under his chin breathing in the scent of him. "I wish." she hesitated. Not knowing exactly what it was that she wished and afraid to voice it if she did.

"I know." he responded, stroking her hair gently. Kelly relaxed into his embrace and sighed. She couldn't see the moisture welling in his eyes as he held her.

That evening Fletch took her to the airport and set her down across from the gate. He refused to say "goodbye." Just "see you later". "Bad luck to say goodbye" he had insisted. "I'll call you when you get in."

Kelly crossed the aisle to stand with the jostling passengers as the boarding process began. She turned for a last look. It was a bittersweet salve to her heart. There he was, shoulder against the wall. Watching her with those penetrating eyes. The wild masculine beauty of him standing there tore at her heart. She felt him withdrawing as she was, into the mode of two professionals again. It was an easy and familiar way of protecting themselves from pain.

Kelly brought the tips of her fingers to her brow in a small salute. Anyone else might have thought she was just brushing back an errant hair. Fletch straightened and brought his hand up in return, a slight smile teasing at the corner of his mouth. It was enough to lighten her spirits.

Kelly turned and walked into the aircraft. She found her seat and snuggled into the warm leather upholstery. The heavy 767 took off in a roar of engines, pressing her against the padding. She felt cradled, safe, and secure. The big jet climbed back up the Potomac River. She noticed that the deep throb of the engines was more comforting, colors seemed more vivid and the face of a child sleeping next to her seemed sweeter than she'd been aware of for a long time. Kelly closed her eyes and slept as the 767 took her to Atlanta.

Fletch stood at the window and watched until the lights of Kelly's aircraft disappeared into the setting sun. When the glow faded, leaving the horizon in darkness, he turned and walked back to his car. The cell phone buzzed against his hip. He unlatched it and looked at the caller ID. He brought the phone reluctantly to his ear. Lt. Colonel Joe Johnson was calling.

"Agent Fletcher here."

"If you want to retain that title Agent Fletcher, you'll listen and you'll listen good." The recriminations flooded out of his phone. He stood there drowning in disbelief. A crushing sense of loss weighed down on him as he realized that his worst fears had come true.

"Are you clear on this Agent Fletcher?" the Intelligence Officer's voice finished at the end of the diatribe. He took Fletch's stunned silence as a "yes". "You've come far too close to compromising this mission." Joe continued. "You established a personal relationship with the subject and gave her information she isn't authorized to have." Before Fletch could object Joe anticipated him by stating, "Where this matter and Kelly Hunter are concerned, you have no private life."

"Sir." Fletch interjected. "I've done what you asked and she identified Rasheed and Wail. I don't know where you think that I have in any way compromised this mission in doing so".

"I know you don't Agent Fletcher." Joe continued. "That's my point exactly. You're too emotionally involved to use good judgment in this case and Kelly Hunter is too savvy a woman not to guess she's a target." There was a brief hesitation before the Intelligence Officer added, "I think that you found that out."

Fletch felt the heat rising in his face as he realized the implications of the last statement. His knuckles turned white as his grip tightened angrily on the phone.

"You've had us under surveillance and bugged my apartment?" Fletch stated in disbelief.

"You're a Federal Agent. You know as well as I do that you don't qualify for the same privacy rights as an ordinary citizen." Joe stated.

"Joe," Fletch began indignantly.

"This case is not up for argument or discussion Fletcher." the voice stated. "May I remind you that not only did you put all of our jobs at risk in this but you can also be brought up on criminal charges for violation of your security clearance."

Fletch was shocked at this turn of events and the vehemence in the Intelligence officer's statements. He felt angry and humiliated. It worried him that there might be some modicum of truth to what Lt. Colonel

Joe Johnson had said. Fletcher's mind felt paralyzed and unable to defend itself.

"There will be no further contact between you and the subject, First Officer Hunter, in any form." the Intelligence officer continued. "No goodbyes. No explanations. Not even so much as a wave in the park. If I were you I'd change any phone number she might have for you. You will go about your duties as a Federal Air Marshall and drop this as of NOW. - Is that understood?"

Fletch knew it was a direct order and not a question. He hated himself for answering "Yes sir." He knew anything else would be a disaster. At least this would buy him time to think.

"Good." the Intelligence officer responded.

"We'll keep an eye on First Officer Hunter." he added in a clumsy attempt at reassurance. "She'll get over it."

There was a moment of silence before Fletch heard a click and a dial tone. He didn't think Kelly would get over it any more than he thought the Feds would protect her. Flipping the phone closed, he braced himself against the door of his car and struggled with despair. It was one of the rare times in his life when he had no idea what to do next. His heart felt like it had followed Kelly into the West leaving him a hollow shell. Still, he wouldn't have traded the last few days for anything.

The Gathering Quiet

The last light drained from the Gulf, leaving a strip of fire fading over the horizon. At Huffman Aviation, the ramp lights flickered across the parked trainers, metal birds resting before the next day's flight. Inside one of the classrooms, a ceiling fan creaked lazily above two men who no longer needed lessons.

Mohammed Atta stood at the whiteboard, erasing weather data he'd written hours ago. The words visibility and ceiling vanished beneath his sleeve. He wasn't interested in flying anymore. He was rehearsing destiny.

Marwan sat near the window, the blue glow of the motel sign cutting across his face. "They're coming soon?" he asked.

Atta nodded without looking up. "All of them. The Brigades of Belief will gather. After that, nothing will ever be the same."

The fan clicked again, its tired blades slicing the humid air. Somewhere beyond the open door, a Cessna engine coughed to life, then fell silent. The sound hung in the night like a held breath.

Outside, the Florida sky darkened into a single, endless shade of gray.

Tomorrow, it would begin.

Bibliography

- PERFECT SOLDIERS: Terry McDermott L.A. Times reporter   "The 9/11 hijackers. Who they were and why they did it' / Published 2002

- STUDIES IN CONFLICT and TERRORISM;: Taylor & Francis Online: Volume 32 Issue 3 published 2009

- PERSONALITY PROFILE OF SEPTEMBER 11 HIJACK RINGLEADER MOHAMMED ATTA: Department of Psychology St. John's University   By Aubrey Immelmann   Paper presented at 25th Scientific meeting of the International Society of Political Psychology. Berlin, Germany   July 16th through July 19th 2002.

- NATIONAL COMMISSION ON TERRORIST ATTACKS ON THE UNITED STATES   : https://govinfo.Library.unt.edu

- AL QAEDA AIMS AT THE UNITED STATES:.   " 5 Terrorists enter the US"

- NOTIFICATION OF APPROVAL OF CHANGE OF STATUS FOR PILOT TRAINING FOR TERRORIST HIJACKERS MOHAMMED ATTA AND…:
House.gov.https://commondocs.house.gov
MARCH 2002

- PART 1 "WE HAVE SOME PLANES" NATIONAL ARCHIVES .gov https://www.archives.gov Aug 26, 2004

- 9/11 HIJACKERS: N.Y. TIMES https://www.nytimes.com

- SIX MONTHS LATER ON MARCH 11 2002 HUFFMAN AVIATION: Department of Justice https://oig.justice.gov

- THE TERRORISTS NEEDED TO DETERMINE THE TECHNIQUES NEEDED TO: National Commission on Terrorist Attacks https://9/11commission.gov

- THE IMMIGRATION AND NATURALIZATION SERVICE CONTACTS WITH 2 SEPTEMBER 11 TERRORISTS: Office of THE INSPECTOR GENERAL

- THE LOOMING TOWER   ROAD TO 9/11 By Lawrence Wright

- Detailed departure log and Statistics chart Boston Logan International Airport on September 11 2001

- FOUR HOURS OF FEAR   9/11S UNTOLD STORY: USA Today August 13 2002

- CLOSE CALL WITH FLIGHT 11: Wareham Courrier September 20th 2001

- FLIGHT #89 AND DAL FLIGHT # 1989 CONFUSION: Warham,   Courrier December 7, 2001

- DELTA FLIGHT 1989 DEPARTURE DETAILS FOR 9/11 : 3TS RECORD

- ATC RECORDING OF 9/11 FLIGHT #93 Transcript.

- CLEARING THE SKIES : USA TODAY 9/11 review December 8 2002

- http://256.com/gray/thoughts/2001/200109 12/delta_flight_1989_9_11/travel.SHTML "TRAVELING   ON   DELTA FLIGHT#1989 ON 9/11"

- SEPTEMBER 11 2001 REVISITED": THE CENTER FOR AN INFORMED AMERICA

- THE CLEVELAND AIRPORT MYSTERY : 9/11 ENCYCLOPEDIA REVISED discussion 2004

- ACRON BEACON JOURNAL : Cleveland Plane Dealer Re: 9/11 DAL flight#1989

- CLEVELAND AIRPORT MYSTERY : Global Free Press http:// 911review.org/invglobalfreepress/Cleveland_airport_mystery.htmz

- 9/11 CONSPIRACY THEORIES Wikipedia

- " GET OUT OF HERE! WHAT ARE YOU DOING?" USA TODAY Delta Airlines 1989 timeline and ATC recording transcript.

- DAL FLIGHT #1989 ABOARD: USA TODAY reporter Robert Hanashiro article on Delta flight #1989 8/13/2002

- DAL FLIGHT 1989 PLANE DIVERTED TO CLEVELAND TRIGGERS ALARM :

THE Plane Dealer   Wednesday, September 12, 2001

- TARGET: AMERICA : TERROR ATTACKS TOUCHED FOLKS ON SOUTH COAST : Sunday Standard Times New Bedford Mass. September 16, 2001

- INTRUDERS IN THE COCKPIT : USA TODAY   by Paul Whyte

- MOHAMMED ATTA'S FLIGHT TRAINING: ERS NEWS

- NATIONAL COMMISSION ON TERRORIST ATTACKS / 9/11 COMISSION REPORT – updated version

- THE EDUCATION OF A HOLY WARRIOR : NYT MAGAZINE By Jeffery Goldberg

- SAUDI DISSIDENT BIN LADEN SEEN AS A SERIOUS THREAT: REUTERS Feb. 25, 1987

- HOW AL QAEDA SCOUTED ATTACKS IN ISRAEL AND EGYPT : New York Times   March 1, 2000

- SOME SEE US AS TERRORIST's NEXT BIG TAEGET : LA Times By John Thor Dahlburg January 13, 2000

- MOHAMMED ATTA : Wikipedia   his Martyrdom video and will

- FBI HIJACKER'S TIMELINE

- 9/11 HAUNTS HIJACKERS SPONSORS. GERMAN COUPLE TALKS ABOUT LIVING WITH ATTA ; Chicago Tribune March 7, 2003

- A FANATIC'S QUIET PATH TO TERROR : Washington Post By Peter Finn September 22, 2001 "Rage was born in Egypt, nurtured in Germany, and inflicted on the U.S.

- UNITED AIRLINES FLIGHT #175 TIMELINE   : https://remember9/11albertarose.org/175 timelineUA_flt_-175_timeline.atm

- US ELITE COUNTERTERRORISM FORCES – S.F. Tomajczyk

- THE MANY FACES OF AL QAEDA : Peter Zeihan July 13, 2007

- Personal Interviews – Delta Air Lines
  Captain Pat Gilmore Re: Mohammad Atta
  Jump seat rider 7/26/2001